The Surprise of Her Life

HELEN R. MYERS

MILLS & BOON®

First published in Great Britain 2012
by Mills & Boon, an imprint of Harlequin (UK) Limited.
Large Print edition 2012
Harlequin (UK) Limited,
Eton House, 18-24 Paradise Road,
Richmond, Surrey TW9 1SR

© Helen R. Myers 2012

ISBN: 978 0 263 23022 2

Harlequin (UK) policy is to use papers that are natural,
renewable and recyclable products and made from
wood grown in sustainable forests. The logging
and manufacturing process conform to the legal
environmental regulations of the country of origin.

Printed and bound in Great Britain
by CPI Antony Rowe, Chippenham, Wiltshire

HELEN R. MYERS

is a collector of two- and four-legged strays, and lives deep in the Piney Woods of East Texas. She cites cello music and bonsai gardening as favorite relaxation pastimes, and still edits in her sleep—an accident, learned while writing her first book. A bestselling author of diverse themes and focus, she is a three-time RITA® Award nominee, winning for *Navarrone* in 1993.

Chapter One

"Oh, *no*— Help!"

Of course, she didn't expect any. Eve Easton had come alone into the kitchen and was reaching into the commercial-size refrigerator with its double, glass doors to pull out the carved-crystal punch bowl, made heavier by pounds of chipped ice and boiled shrimp. But just when she turned toward the counter, the unwieldy thing had started slipping from her grasp.

Miracle of miracles, strong arms wrapped

around hers in support, and a mellow, male voice assured her, "Got it."

Too relieved to have avoided catastrophe to yelp from surprise that someone had actually heard her, Eve held her breath as, together, she and her mystery hero jointly hoisted the thing to the counter. Unfortunately, their combined momentum made it land with a sharp thud.

"Don't shatter," she entreated the bowl. "Glass shards aren't a digestible garnish." That was the problem with helping out here; everything in the place was genuine, gorgeous and breakable.

"Do you always reprimand inanimate objects?"

As her foolishness sunk in, she chuckled self-consciously—feeling increasingly so for their awkward positioning. "Oh, ignore me. I've spent most of my life either swimming upstream, ignoring logic, or otherwise trying to defy physics."

"Eve? Eve Prescott… It *is* you."

Already remaining stiff enough to shatter herself, Eve willed herself to faint. She was 99.99 percent sure she wasn't dreaming, so there was no other escape from this moment. And the man who held her against the counter so tightly that they were as close as two people could get—short of sexual intimacy—sounded eerily similar to one of three people she'd hoped never to see again in this lifetime. The fact that he addressed her by her married name confirmed the impossible had happened.

God, leaving Texas wasn't enough? In case you've forgotten, you don't let Southwest fly to Mars yet.

Lifting her gaze to stare at their reflection in the glass cabinets at the end of the kitchen counter, she managed to eke out on a thin breath, "It's Easton now, Mr. Roland. I took back my maiden name." She didn't dare turn her head what with him being so close, his breath already a lover's caress against her ear and cheek.

"Of course. Sorry."

It was then that his gaze lifted, seeming to follow hers, and they were staring at each other in the glass. "What are you doing here?" she asked him.

"I was invited—well—by a friend of an invited guest. Then by our hostess herself when my friend checked with her."

Responding literally to her question also confirmed her conclusion—like she needed that. Derek Roland was nothing if not a stick-to-the-facts guy. What else would you expect from a government man? "I meant what are you doing in Colorado? Wait. First, would you mind—?" She bobbed her head to the right, signaling him to let go and give her some space. "If we get any closer, you'll be able to describe my birthmark."

With an understated clearing of his throat, he

did exactly that, stepping around the kitchen bar to grasp the back of a brass-and-wood chair instead. "I live here now. Apparently you do, as well, or are you visiting relatives? You don't resemble either of the Graingers."

Wearing a new champagne-colored cashmere dress that felt like a second skin—something she intended to let Rae Grainger know was *not* her best wardrobe recommendation to date—Eve ran her hands over her hips where she could still feel his body heat. Yes, it was him—Derek Roland. Mr. Tall, Groomed and Stern. Even the perpetual frown between his eyebrows was exactly as she remembered; nevertheless, he was an attractive man, and she didn't actually hold any resentment toward him. To be fair, she'd concluded him to be as much an injured party to what had occurred as she was. His offense was simply to be here and, therefore, was a reminder of the humiliation she'd fled Texas to forget.

"I'm not related to either Rae or Gus," she replied, acutely aware of the visual study he was conducting of her. "Rae is my boss. *Denver Events Planning.*"

"From PTA fairy godmother and Booster Club organizer to events planner. That makes all the sense in the world and probably keeps you as busy as ever. You have to love the wardrobe upgrade?"

"It's…different." And keeping busy was the idea. She'd needed to stay as active as possible during her awake hours so she didn't drown in a pity party for one when she should be sleeping. The paycheck was the other motivator to keep at this. "You're absolutely right, though, I'm not qualified for much else," she admitted ruefully.

"I didn't mean—"

"Did you transfer to the Denver office, Mr. Roland?" she asked before he could finish. Back in Texas he'd been the most whispered-about person on their block. It wasn't every day you had an FBI agent as a neighbor.

"Please, make that Derek, and, yes, something like that. I'm the S.A.C. here."

"Excuse me, I'm terrible with abbreviations."

"Special Agent-in-Charge."

"Oh. *Oh.* Wow. Congratulations." Without trying, he'd succeeded in making her feel even younger and less accomplished than she already did.

The stereotype continued to hold true; even in his gray suit and two-tone silver tie, he looked "government," just as he had back in Texas when he and his then-wife Sam had moved in next door to her and Wes. It was when she brought over a peach cobbler she'd baked herself that Samantha Roland confided that *her* Derek was with "the Agency." Derek had always struck Eve as a serious man, and you'd have to be obtuse not to notice that his job demanded much of his time. He'd almost never been around for small talk, even when outside mowing the lawn or cleaning up the branch-littered yard after a strong storm. Every chore or project was achieved at a brisk pace that suggested he had more important things to do and places to be. They were speaking more now than they had in all of the time that they'd been neighbors.

Eve doubted that she could bring herself to call him by his first name. He might only be five or so years her senior, but his whole bearing made her feel a full decade deficit in experience. "Rae will be thrilled," she assured him, with a death hold on her role as assistant to one of the most talked-about women in Denver. "I think you've managed to put a new feather in her cap. With the weather as unrelenting as it is, I know she's grateful if the D.A. or a judge will come up here. It's usually the show business and sports people who are brave enough to take on the mountains in these conditions."

"I'm glad I could make it. The place is spectacular." As he spoke, Derek gave the state-of-the-art yet creative room a more thorough and admiring look. "I actually came with D.A. Maines."

She literally bit her tongue to avoid saying, "Oh," and spread her hands in a well-there-you-have-it gesture. If D.A. Maines remembered her, it would be as the coat check girl, when she'd actually handed him a program and glass of champagne at the pre-party to the opening of the theater's yearly premiere of *The Nutcracker* ballet.

"His wife is with their daughter on a school-related trip to Italy, and he wasn't up for ringing in the New Year with a TV dinner and case files."

Never mind trying to picture the district attorney eating a frozen dinner, Eve had to force her gaze from Derek's mouth. Slightly curved into a smile, his lips weren't as thin as she used to believe, now that they weren't fixed in that tight, white line they usually were back in Texas. In fact they seemed kind, and—tempting.

"You cut your hair."

The unexpected observation had her self-consciously smoothing the short wisps at her nape. A year ago, her naturally blond locks had almost reached her waist. "There's an understatement if I ever heard one. My ex—and probably yours—would say that I look scalped."

"You look…great. Very chic, or is that an archaic expression these days?"

At first, she'd worried that the style made her look like a street urchin out of *Oliver Twist,* but heartened by his seemingly sincere admiration a bit of her impish humor surfaced. "Full disclosure? All I was doing was indulging a little immature spite. Typical southern male, Wes would complain at the slightest trimming I'd do to get rid of split ends."

The truth was, once past her high school cheerleading years, she felt the weight of her hair too much for her slight frame. The first thing she did, after finding the apartment in Denver, was to walk into a full-service salon and ask for it all to be cut off. It not only felt liberating in ways she hadn't imagined, but donating her shorn locks to an organization that would turn it into a wig for a child with cancer gave her a quiet joy. Interestingly, her migraine-size headaches soon stopped, too.

"I can top that." Derek pretended to glance around before sliding her a conspiratorial look. "As I was moving out, I came upon Samantha's engagement ring in the bathroom. I 'accidentally' flipped it into the commode."

Eve couldn't keep from sucking in her breath at the image. Sam's ring was only half the size of Rae's, but it was one hundred percent more than Eve had ever worn. Too grateful for this moment to resist, she asked, "Did she notice before...you know?"

With a negligent shrug, he replied, "She must have, she signed the divorce papers."

Eve laughed with relief. Incredible, she thought, they were actually making small talk—and it was *fun*. The few times they'd exchanged greetings back in Texas, she'd hesitated and stuttered like a nine-year-old, finding herself in front of the school principal.

"Are you liking Colorado?" she ventured.

"So far, so good, although it took me a while to adjust to the altitude."

"As physically fit as you people have to be?" Eve didn't hide her surprise. "I thought I was going to have to buy my own personal oxygen tank. And it was a good thing I wasn't wearing a ring anymore because my fingers swelled like sausages on a grill."

Derek's answering glance exposed his

amusement but disbelief. "I knew you'd moved, Eve. I just had no idea it was here. I hope this isn't too awkward for you, but I was merely looking for a secluded spot to check my BlackBerry for calls without appearing rude or attracting too much attention."

Sensing he was turning back into FBI Agent Roland, Eve pointed to the sunroom at the back of the kitchen. It was a rather romantic nook with the outdoor lights from the patio twinkling through the floor-to-ceiling windows. "Consider me gone. If you need more light, there's a switch to your left as soon as you enter. You'll have the kitchen to yourself. I'm off to deliver this," she said, gesturing to the bowl that had started their conversation.

Frowning, he reached out to stay her retreat. "Give me a second and I'll carry that beast for you."

With that he removed the BlackBerry from its belt clip, exposing his badge, and focused on the small screen. After only a few seconds and fewer clicks, he replaced it.

"Lead the way," he said, reaching for the heavy receptacle.

She did, acutely aware of his gaze following her every step. Although she thought she looked the best she had in a year, she would have passed on this glove of a dress if not for Rae's insistence when they'd gone on a shopping spree together. Granted, she'd admitted that she was frustrated with her harmless, girl-next-door image, but blatant-vamp persona felt a ridiculous reach. Angelina Jolie in *The Tourist*, she wasn't. But the knee-length dress was a contradiction, as well. It had a demure, high front, but Derek had the real view—a seriously low, cowl neck in back exposing just about every inch of her from nape to waist, all of which was prickling—and not because the temperature in the house was too low. She wasn't a gambler, but she could feel Derek's gaze contemplating what she was and wasn't wearing beneath the thing.

At the long buffet in the dining room, Eve indicated the spot where the bowl should go and stepped aside for him to put his hefty load in its place. "I do appreciate this," she said as discreetly as she could, counting how many pairs of eyes had noticed.

"My pleasure. Besides, that dress doesn't look like anything you can machine wash and I'm fast concluding that eau de shrimp isn't the right fragrance for you."

She heard a few chuckles from people over-hearing the exchange and felt a betraying heat creep into her face. Special Agent Roland was flirting…with *her.* The man whom she last saw angry enough to bite inch-thick bolts in two when he'd come to confront Wes about his affair with Samantha. She couldn't begin to wrap her mind around that idea.

"Eve, introduce me to this gallant gentleman," Rae said, joining them. "I thought I'd greeted all of our guests, but I'm obviously remiss in welcoming you," she added to Derek. She extended her beautifully manicured hand in a way that best displayed her French-tipped fingernails and several carats of diamonds.

Almost as tall as Derek and luscious in a silver-sequined, full-length gown, Rae's personality was cranked tonight to radiate mach charm. Her reputation in Denver was at once admired and resented due to her ambition and fearlessness. She never questioned her taste or decisions and if a client did, they didn't need to hire Rae Grainger for their function. That matched her bold appearance—flaming red hair and matching lips, permanent liner and eyebrows, and teeth that any TV personality would kill for.

With wry circumspection that played well to her brashness, Derek picked up a napkin, wiped his right hand and took hers.

"Mrs. Grainger. Thank you for allowing me to join you."

"You don't look like a golfing buddy or business associate of my husband's. And you have better manners."

"More like an associate of D.A. Maines, who is taking pity on someone relatively new in town. Derek Roland."

Rae's face radiated her recognition and she nodded approvingly, which almost ended suspiciously like a royal bow. "I remember now. How lovely to have you, Special Agent-in-Charge Roland."

Eve resisted the urge to roll her eyes by respecting her incredible memory. Rae could recite event quotes, guest lists and her daily phone log from a month back.

"Call me Derek, please…unless I come bearing a warrant."

With a throaty laugh, Rae replied, "Well, *Derek,* you are obviously blessed with as much good taste as you are with chivalry and wit. I've about given myself an ulcer at the idea of all this loveliness going to waste." As she spoke, she swept her hand toward Eve.

For the briefest moment, Eve thought the groan in her mind actually burst from her lips. But unable to stay silent out of fear total humiliation was forthcoming, she stage-whispered, "This was my former *neighbor,* Rae. *My* ex and *his* are now *married.*"

Rarely rattled, the resilient redhead muttered a brief, "Crap" through a frozen smile.

"Or something to that effect," Eve muttered, wishing for a glass of anything to swig down. Crawling under the twenty-thousand-dollar dining table was out of the question. "I'm going to get the last of the sushi now," she said to the room at large. "With luck, I'll trip along the way, knock myself out and come to with amnesia."

Once back in the kitchen, she leaned her

forehead against the cool glass of the refrigerator. What had she done to deserve this? Even though Derek was being an absolute gentleman, he *was* a reminder of everything she'd been trying to put behind her, namely her failure as a wife and as a woman.

Hearing the door creak open behind her, she quickly made her way to the sink where she pumped soap into her palm and then ran water to wash her hands before setting to work again. She wasn't surprised to see Derek's image suddenly reflected beside hers in the sink window.

"Are you okay?" he asked.

"Sure. This happens to me every day."

"You don't sound okay."

"Well, don't take this personally, but having all but cried my way through Christmas because I missed my family and we were too busy to get time off to fly down to see them, the last thing I needed was my past hitting me in the face like a tacky pie-throwing joke."

As she witnessed Derek's head rear back as though she'd struck him on the chin, Eve grimaced and turned to face him. "I didn't mean *you*. I meant the affair and everything. You've been all kindness. But you don't know Rae. She may have appeared apologetic, but she's taking your consideration to me the wrong way, as she will your presence. Trust me, regardless of what I said, or will say, she's got an idea in her head and she will Frankenstein monster it into—I don't want to think what."

If he was upset at that news, Derek didn't show it. Instead, he ripped off a sheet from the paper towel roll beside him and handed it to her.

"Oh, good grief, see? I'm dripping all over the hardwood floor and myself."

"I wish you weren't so uncomfortable about our reunion," he said as she dried her hands, blotted her skirt and quickly dabbed at the few drops on the floor.

"You aren't?"

"Not at all. I remember you as lovely in all ways, and I felt as badly for you as I did for myself. More actually."

His flattery was as potent as wine and she was grateful for the need to turn her back on him so she could toss the paper towel in the trash compactor. "Why? You don't know me. Maybe I deserved what happened. Do you realize this is the longest conversation we've had in all the time we were neighbors?"

"My work requires me to read people well."

Thinking of his choice in marriage partners, she spun around. "I have two words for you and her initials are—"

"Resist that one." Derek came an inch away from touching his index finger to her lips before stopping himself. "I don't want to be remotely tempted to speak *your* ex's name in rebuttal."

As he continued to be transfixed by her lips,

Eve grasped at humor as she always did when finding herself in an uncomfortable moment. "Hey, *I* never said I'm a good judge of character. I'm always surprised when people don't mess up or let me down. Take my mother for example—I counted on her to produce another sibling so I wouldn't be stuck being the baby of the family and forever being treated as if I have packing bubble for brains and shouldn't be let outside after dark. But did she follow through? Nope."

His tender smile was a dirty trick. It transformed his face in a way that made her tummy tighten and her heart flutter. In self-defense, Eve circled the island the long way around to take the plastic wrapping off of the last two trays.

"I have to get the rest of this sushi out there," she told him.

"Let me take it," Derek said. "No doubt you've been going nonstop since before this party started. Sit down. Breathe. I'll bring us back a glass of something. Do you prefer bubbles or ice?"

He intended to prolong this? After a moment of dread, she had to admit she would be grateful to delay Rae's inevitable questions. "Neither," she forced herself to say. "If there's any Cabernet or Pinot Noir open, that would be nice."

He left before Eve could change her mind.

If only she could sneak out the back door and leave. However, having arrived early this afternoon, she knew her SUV was undoubtedly blocked in several times over. The plan had been for her to spend the night in one of the guest rooms.

Feeling trapped and so off balance that she was starting to scratch at her wrist, then her neck, she withdrew to the little garden table in the sunroom. "No hives," she commanded herself. "Please no hives."

The coolness and darkness enveloped and soothed her. Just these few yards even cut the sound of the revelry going on in the other parts of the house.

Breathe.

"Where did you go?"

He had returned quickly, Eve thought, or else she'd managed to zone out longer than she'd imagined. "Back here," she called, raising her hand to wave. She hadn't turned on the sunroom light and knew she was concealed in the shadows.

"Nice," he said, setting the two fat goblets of dark red wine on the glass table. He eased onto the diminutive iron garden chair that faced her. "Is this thing going to take my weight?"

"It manages Gus's. He and Rae often have coffee or wine here. Rae made this set herself." Eve enjoyed Derek's startled look. "Physically, she may trigger thoughts of a flashy bird-of-paradise blossom, and heaven knows that's her personality, but she's as serious a craftsman in her free time as she is a businesswoman."

"Great praise considering that you sounded like you wanted to take clippers to those French nails of hers for her attempted match-making."

The man saw entirely too much for her peace of mind. "Rae has no sense of boundaries where her affections are concerned. She expects us to recognize that what she does is for our own good. Just ask Gus," Eve added with a chuckle. "But she's been the equivalent of that college degree I never got as she's mentored me. And she's generous to a fault."

"Then I'm glad you found her. Has this been your first position since moving up here?"

"My second, actually. My first was a secretarial position in the front office of the Broncos, but that was all too much of a reminder of what I'd just left." Trying to think of a segue out of this line of conversation, she stroked the cool edge of the smooth goblet. Glass was one of her favorite mediums, but she had no artistic passion to do something creative herself. She was beginning to wonder if she had any passion whatsoever. She had Wes to thank for that self-doubt, as well.

"Doesn't the D.A. want a little of your time?" she asked a little too brightly. "I thought when someone invites you to something like this, it's because there are things they want to talk about. Or there's someone you needed assistance in meeting at the function."

As he tasted his wine, Derek's gray eyes lit with amusement. "That's mostly the case in fiction when you have to fill the pages between action scenes. If it wasn't for my swollen ego, I'd worry that you're trying to get rid of me."

"No," she lied. "But I just wanted you to know that I understood if you wanted to get back to mingling or—I don't know what's off-

limits to talk about given your job?" *Our past. Did you ever have a clue as to what was going on? Was Wes as friendly to you as Sam was to me pretending that everything was normal?*

"Ask what you'd like—except for the number of the red phone on the president's desk. Also, if there really are aliens at Area 51."

Suddenly, Eve got it—she was fluff to him. Harmless. Her makeover may have upgraded her sex appeal, but he undoubtedly knew better and just saw her as an easy route to getting through his own difficult holiday break before returning to his *real* world. That compelled her to ask a question that would have annoyed her if their places were reversed.

"Have you heard anything from Samantha since your divorce?"

"No," he said, without hesitation. "But I'd made it clear to her that I expected not to, except through our attorneys. Are you hoping to hear from Wes?"

"Good grief, no. I think that's the one thing that would make my family disown me."

"Whatever it takes," he mused.

While his lips curved in that appealing way, Eve thought she read something in his smoke-colored eyes that made her think of secrets. She grew immediately apprehensive. "But you...know...something?"

"Eve, it's New Year's. Do you really want to do this?"

"The fool got fired, didn't he? It serves him right. I was always baking brownies and fried pies to soothe the assistant coaches he'd offend—"

"I hear through reliable sources that our exes are expecting."

She didn't gasp, she had that much control. But otherwise, Eve was shocked into just staring at him.

"There lies the lesson," Derek said quietly, almost apologetic. "Sometimes flirting with the idea that you want information ends up teaching you that you don't."

Summoning what pride she could, she straightened her spine and squared her shoulders and insisted, "I'm only surprised at how fast it happened."

"I suspect, being several years older than you, Samantha's biological clock was sounding like Big Ben's toll to her."

"You didn't want children?" she asked, without thinking.

His look was enigmatic, but he replied, "A child isn't always the solution to problems."

Eve looked out into the magical night and watched the lights twinkle on the shrubbery and trees. "I'm so clueless, I didn't know we had problems. We were married for almost eight years, and I believed him when he reasoned that we should wait before starting a family." Until he had job security, then it was a larger nest egg, then it was something else.

"Well, if money was one of the reasons, they don't have that concern now. I gave Sam the house, and she'll get close to half of my pension to date."

Eve slid him a sympathetic look. "You were very generous."

After something close to a growl, he replied, "Legally, there wasn't much I could do about the pension, and I ended up giving her my equity in the house to keep from having to liquidate a few other things that I inherited from my side of the family."

"You don't have anyone left, do you? I think I remember Sam saying you were an only child, too?"

"That's right."

"Thankfully all of my family is still alive." Eve almost felt guilty for having so much when he had so little. What's more, she had a reliable vehicle and a modest nest egg from her share of the equity that had come from the sale of their house, and Wes's college debt was paid off. "I'm sorry that you have to think about Wes living in your house."

"That happens less than you might think."

Seeing his eyes try to hold her gaze, she admitted, "You know, back when we were neighbors, I was intimidated by you. So much so that I delayed going outside if you were mowing or something."

He leaned forward and offered a conspiratorial, "We train to have that effect on people. Keeps everyone but reporters and politicians at arm's length." Lifting his glass again he waited for her to lift hers and gently touched rim to rim. "Allow me to make amends."

Eve's heart skittered at his subtle flirtation. "Amends" were not necessary and those feelings were part of a past she really was trying to put behind her. On top of that, she reminded herself, while he was handling her with kid gloves, she was still being *handled*. He'd admitted as much. He was a control-oriented man. Hadn't she just divorced one of those? Maybe Wes was an amateur compared to someone trained by a government agency, but Wes had carried some clout in their community as he'd risen to the post of head coach of consistently winning football, basketball and baseball teams. Increasingly, he'd carried that persona home with him. She'd parried it with some success through her sense of humor and the reminder that "For better or worse" didn't necessarily mean illness, it meant someone dropping the ball relationship-wise. No, hindsight told her that she hadn't been completely blindsided by the divorce.

"You have to appease my curiosity," Derek said, breaking into her thoughts. "What brought you to Colorado? I think Samantha said you were born and raised in Texas."

"That's true. All of the senior members of the family live near a retirement community north of Houston. That's where both sets of my grandparents are. My parents joke that they live off campus." At Derek's surprised look, she grinned with pleasure. "Yeah, the Eastons and Leelands are a bunch of tough old birds. Plus I have an older brother, Nicholas, in Houston. He's a cardiac surgeon, and my middle sibling, Sela, is a corporate attorney in San Antonio. To answer your question, I just needed some space. It's true that my grandparents are getting frail, but I thought I could catch a flight anytime and spend a long weekend with everyone. What I didn't count on was how busy Rae would keep me. And I must admit the cold makes me question part of my decision. Don't get me wrong, I like the outdoors but winters aren't as long in Texas as they are here."

"You've got that right. Do you ski?"

She couldn't quite stifle a giggle as she thought of her answer. "I'm deemed expert

on the kids' beginner slope, and I've humiliated myself twice by taking the 360-degree
excursion tour via the lift to the adult slope.
Just ask Rae and Gus."

"I could cure that."

Wow, Eve thought, when the man wanted to
make a point, he didn't mince words. "Short
of threatening me with arrest for scaring children and wildlife with my screams, I doubt it."

Derek's look was as intimate as it was confident. "That I'd never do."

Once again she felt things she had no business feeling around this man. Eve was certain
that he didn't really mean to sound seductive,
but an undeniable chemistry had spawned
between them. What a surprise, considering
his deceptively conventional appearance. His
square-jawed, slightly off-angle face denied
him classical handsomeness the way his loose-
fitting suit almost hid that he was a man of
strength. Having glimpsed his badge as he'd

tucked away his BlackBerry, she supposed the cut of his clothing was to hide what else that belt carried. She'd seen him in shorts and his legs were powerful and well shaped. Even tall Sam must have felt tiny wrapped in his arms.

"Well, either way," she said, grateful for the darkness that hopefully hid her blush, "you'd be wasting your time."

"Then you should try cross-country skiing with me. I actually like it better. Shorter skis, and you can pick the difficulty of your terrain. Plus it's more private," he added at her doubtful look. "Few people to see any mishaps."

Her traitorous imagination pictured them in a secluded part of the woods, her sandwiched between him and a great old pine, him unzipping her jacket and caressing and kissing her until she couldn't feel the cold anymore.

She shook her head to stop the images. "Skidding across the supermarket parking lot is as adventurous as I'm willing to get these days. Trust me, I'm too boring for you."

"Says who? Wes the Wonderful, who needed to collect more than sports trophies to feel good about himself?"

Although his tone wasn't unkind, the sting of truth had Eve swallowing hard. She raised her glass in salute, even though she wasn't sure her hand would be steady. "You've got me, G-man. I guess a new dress does not a bruised ego fix."

"It's New Year's and whether you're into resolutions or not, at least let your hair down for the evening. Figuratively speaking," he added, giving her cute do another admiring glance. "That's a great song they're playing out there, can you hear it?"

She could. She was woefully behind with new titles and singers, but she loved this classic. "Etta James singing 'At Last.'"

"Ma'am." Derek rose and formally bowed as

he extended his hand. "These are close quarters, but would you care to shuffle?"

Why not? she thought, liking him more with each surprising disclosure into his character. She also was touched at how he was trying to make her feel comfortable around him. Unable to deny the invitation in his eyes, Eve placed her hand in his and rose. "Brave man risking a trip to the E.R. tonight."

His chest shook in laughter as they stepped toward each other in that little cool nook bathed in muted light and surrounded by Rae's pots of herbs. Their addictive scents added to the ambience as man and woman rocked gently to the romantic jazz. In her heels, Eve's temple barely reached his freshly shaven, strong jaw, and yet her hand, engulfed in his, felt like she was cocooned in peace. It was intriguing to discover that someone larger than Wes, and in a more serious line of work, could exhibit so much more tenderness.

"You're one surprise after another," she murmured, letting her eyes close. "I'm going to remember this."

"I damn well hope so."

She chuckled softly at his mock indignation. "Do you sing?"

"Now you're pushing your luck."

As he spoke, his breath subtly moved her bangs and tickled her forehead. She realized she wouldn't have minded if they were his lips. "Do you mind if I do?"

"Are you kidding? Was Tom Hanks ever crazy enough to say no to Meg Ryan?"

Softly, Eve crooned the next stanza.

"Lady, you have soul in your genes." Derek stopped and coaxed her chin up so he could see her face. "I want to hear more."

But there was no more music. The stereo went silent and someone turned up the TV to play the countdown to the New Year. Eve and Derek looked at each other. Despite the distance, the cacophony threatened to shatter the fragile web of magic between them. Time had passed more quickly than either of them realized and caught them in a particularly unexpected and potentially complicated situation.

"Five…four…three…two…one…*Happy New Year!*"

"Happy New Year," he murmured, his gaze roaming over her face.

"And to you," Eve whispered. She grew sad as she felt this sweet, unexpected moment coming to an end.

But instead of releasing her, Derek slowly lowered his head and touched his lips to hers. The caress was warm and gentle. He made her feel delicate and special. Before she could reason herself out of the impulse, Eve kissed him back.

With a sigh of relief, or gratitude, he slid his arms around her again, only this time he brought her closer. Nevertheless, it felt as right as when they were dancing. Then he slanted his mouth over hers, seeking a deeper connection.

"Eve?" Rae called as she swept into the kitchen. "Have you seen Special A—? Oh… and there you are!"

Chapter Two

Eve and Derek separated like guilty teen-
agers caught by their parents. Well, *she* did,
which gave Derek little choice but to release
her. She automatically smoothed her hands
over her dress, while miserably watching Rae
pat her hands together as though she'd just hit
the jackpot at Vegas.

"Do you need me to bring out something?"
she asked.

"No, no. Apologies, darling," the redhead all
but gushed. "I just had to tell Special Agent-

in-Charge Roland that we need to arrange for a ride for him. The district attorney's neighbor's house is on fire, and he rushed off to make sure all is well at his home. He sends his deep regrets," she added to Derek. "Eve dear, I'm thinking *you* should handle this, since you and Derek are longtime friends."

As Rae began bobbing her head up and down for emphasis, Eve started shaking hers. Leave the party with Derek Roland? They'd only been alone for a little while and look what had already happened! Besides that, she wasn't about to drive down this mountain at night with the road still mostly covered in packed snow and ice. She was barely competent at driving in the stuff down on the flats.

"Rae, did you forget that I was to stay and help Carmella clean up?" she asked, referring to the Graingers' live-in housekeeper.

Rae dismissed that technicality with a flick of her hand. "If I can't adjust to a little unexpected glitch like this, I'm in the wrong business, aren't I? Not to worry, dearest. We'll get things taken care of. Enjoy the reunion, you two and—*Happy* New Year."

She dashed away before Eve could think of another reason her presence was vital. That left her and Derek in awkward silence.

This was definitely a night for reality checks, she thought with increasing embarrassment. "I can't decide whether she thought she was helping, or being sarcastic," Eve told him. "I'll go explain that she was wrong about what she thinks she saw."

"What was it then?"

The question, as much as the way he was watching her, left Eve at a loss. She hadn't meant to offend him. All she'd intended to say was that she'd gotten caught up in the moment. Rae might have even done her a favor before she'd made a bigger fool of herself.

"You don't have to feel obligated about the

ride," Derek said, suddenly reaching for his BlackBerry. "I'll call for a cab."

To come all the way up here tonight of all nights? "The aspens will leaf out before you have any luck with that plan," she told him, resigned to what had to be. "Rae's right. I'll take you." It was the only principled thing to do. Tomorrow, Eve told herself, tomorrow she would talk to Rae. Explain that what she saw was just a bit of late-night craziness on top of a hectic schedule and too little rest or food. "Let me get started on loading the dishwasher." Back in pragmatic mode, she felt more in control of herself. "We'll have to wait a few minutes anyway, until some guests leave and there's access to my car."

It was closer to an hour before that became possible, but it passed quickly with Derek insisting on doing his share to help. Eve didn't know whether to be flattered or wonder if he was staying close because he suspected that she might change her mind and abandon him, too?

Finally, after saying a formal good-night to the Graingers and the die-hard partiers, Eve led the way to her red SUV. Only a few steps out the front door and—despite the salt they'd spread earlier—she slipped on some resilient ice. Thanks to Derek's fast reflexes and strength, he saved her from a nasty backward fall.

"Those heels are suicidal. You should have brought boots to change into." His breath creating puffs of vapor in the frigid night air that floated around the faux-fur trim of her red parka telling her what she already knew, since his hands were clasped tightly to her waist and her back was flush to his torso. He was leaning close trying to see her face. But now that they were more alone than ever, she couldn't risk looking into those soul-searching, shaman eyes of his.

"I did. They're still in my suitcase," she said, pointing at her vehicle. "I didn't think I'd need them or my case until later."

"This is just not turning out to be your night, is it?" he said wryly.

He didn't know the half of it, she thought, as they continued on toward the SUV. However, as she began to key the door locks, she knew she couldn't continue this way. "Full disclosure," she blurted out. "I'm an insurance agent's dream customer. Not so much as a driving citation, let alone a fender bender on my record. But the other reason I wanted to stay here tonight and help out wasn't because of you. It was to avoid driving down this mountain in the dark. On the cliff side of the road, no less." She held out her keys to him as though they were toxic. "Even if you didn't go through one of those wild defensive driving courses I've heard they give you guys…would you mind? And feel free to resist confessing if your own driving record is the worst in the Bureau's," she quickly added.

"It isn't." The speed with which Derek took possession indicated that he'd been trying hard not to suggest this solution from the moment they'd stepped outside. "Let me get your door," he said, all solicitude and reassurance. Keeping his arm around her, he succeeded in getting her safely inside.

When they were both settled and he had the engine purring, she fastened her seat belt, turned on her seat's warmer. Then she basically continued with all of the little fussing movements that came with the reality that their close confines felt more intimate than the sunroom did.

"I think I've lost feeling in a few toes," she said, leaning forward to watch as she wriggled them in the strappy shoes.

"I should have carried you," Derek said. "It would have been faster and safer."

The idea of being in his arms again heated her body faster than the heater could. "You're kind, but tongues will be wagging enough as it is."

She could feel his sidelong glance and just knew a question was coming; however, it didn't. Relieved, Eve prepared herself for the nerve-wracking descent.

As they started down the winding road, Eve was surprised to see that although there had been several people leaving at the same time, she could see only one car ahead of them. Everything else was dark, including most of the other houses tucked into the mountainside. By day she loved this area, loved the way nature crafted art via location and climate into every tree, the way sun and shadows played tricks on the eyes making you see things that weren't there, and forced you to pay closer attention to not miss what was. But at this hour, all she saw was the sweep of snow cutting downhill and its steepness made her stomach roil.

In self-defense, she half turned to face Derek. "Don't think I'm staring," she told him. "I'm simply trying to avoid dealing with what's behind me."

"I have to ask, just to reassure myself—is there a panic attack issue you need to tell me about?" Although he frowned, and didn't take his eyes off the road, there was amusement in his voice. "I don't have to worry about you grabbing the wheel or anything, do I?"

"I don't think I'm that far gone. Unless we skid." Please don't skid. *Please don't skid.* But he was handling the machine beautifully, so far successfully avoiding every patch of ice.

"Why don't you tell me about that birthmark?"

"That *what?*" Belatedly, Eve remembered her earlier remark when he'd first entered the kitchen. "Oh! That was just...comedic relief."

"I'm crushed."

Eve wished she had the courage to turn forward again, but was afraid that if she did, she would lose what little she'd eaten this evening. She chose her second-best option—to duck deeper into her jacket like a shy turtle. "I'm not really the flirt you're taking me for." Of all the people she'd had to make a fool of herself in front of, why did it have to be him?

"Doubly crushed."

"Seriously. I'm the dumped wife, remember? Sex appeal in the negatives."

"Right. Which is why, in hindsight, I found myself wishing Rae had taken a wrong turn instead of locating us as quickly as she did." Shifting slightly in his seat, he abruptly added, "This might sound like bitterness, since I'm the rejected party, as well, but I don't owe Sam squat, let alone allegiance, and hadn't for some time. So let me just say this for what it's worth.

Wes is a fool…and that's on top of being the four-letter equivalent of excrement."

Eve waited for more, but Derek, erudite man that he was, said nothing else. "Feel better now?" she ventured to ask.

"I do, actually." After a few moments, he added, "I wish you did."

"I'm getting better." At his brief, disbelieving look, she added, "It's not like I'm hoping he'll waken one morning to the revelation that he made a mistake."

"I should bleeping hope not."

It was sweet of him to be so sensitive to her battered ego. But despite his comment about loyalty undeserving, she couldn't completely shake the nagging concern that all this attention to her was because he harbored a little fantasy about exacting a bit of revenge against one or both of their former mates. Eve inwardly shook her head at how she had become her worst enemy.

In took less than twenty minutes until the worst of their descent was over. In that time, Eve carefully kept questions away from personal matters. She asked if he supervised a large group of people, and he told her that including clerical staff, they had just under two hundred agents.

"There's roughly the same number of specialists, analysts and pro staff. Then there's the different task forces."

"Good grief, you're a king with your own kingdom," she said, intimidated all over again.

When they could see the highway that would take them back to the city, she looked for signs of smoke, or—worse yet—flames, indicating D.A. Maines's situation had grown dire. "I'm sorry I didn't voice more concern over the D.A. Will you be able to call him and see how things are over there?"

"Yeah, I'll check as soon as I get home." Derek turned onto the interstate. The lights from Denver's skyline painted a glittery landscape and stark contrast to the wooded foothills. "If anyone is going to get a fast response from the fire department, it's his neighborhood, but I don't blame him for hurrying off. I would have done the same thing."

"I've met him only a few times, but he seems quite the family man."

"That's the impression I got."

As they passed a series of restaurants, she almost pointed one out to mention that it was particularly good if he liked Thai cuisine. Then she decided against that. He'd been living here almost as long as she had and probably knew about it. And the last thing she wanted was for him to be thinking that she was hinting at an invitation.

He did get her attention when he turned onto a road that she would have taken to get home. When he took the next left, she looked at him with disbelief. But it was when he turned into her apartment complex that she tensed with unease.

"What are you doing?"

"What do you mean?" Pulling into a parking spot in front of the first building, he gave her a wary look. "Are you okay?"

No, she wasn't okay. He was freaking her out. "This is a joke, right?"

Derek pointed to the corner apartment of the building directly in front of them. "'E.T. go home,'" he recited, using a forlorn voice.

No. "You're serious? You live there—since—?"

"Since I arrived in Colorado. It'll be a year in March." He pointed to the black SUV parked in the spot next to him. "That's mine. Why?"

Her heart sinking, Eve reached over to shut off the ignition and pulled out her keys. She used them to point to the building diagonally across from his, specifically the bottom corner apartment. "That's me," she said.

Derek glanced from her to the point of her direction and back again. Then his chest started to shake on a soft laugh. "Well. Hello, neighbor...again."

Derek meant to bring a little levity into the moment, considering that this was playing out to be a classic case of fate having the last laugh. But one look at Eve Easton's adorable, but horrified face, and his smile waned. Damn, but the cutie was hard on his ego. The situation wasn't as awful as all that...was it?

"Okay," he began slowly, "you don't think this is even the slightest bit amusing?"

"More like a bad dream."

"Thanks a lot."

Eve had the grace to wince. "Excuse me. I didn't mean—"

"That you were appalled at the idea of living next door to me? And here I thought that lovely little interlude we shared in the sun-room would be—"

"This would be a good time to start forgetting that."

"Why on earth would I want to? Tonight was the best time I've had since moving here. Come to think of it, it's the best New Year's Eve I've had in…long enough," he said, realizing he was already giving away too much. She'd already managed to deflate him; there was no point in proving that not only did his love life suck, his determination to make high marks with his superiors had turned him into a workaholic. "The point is I'd hoped we'd gotten past that your-ex-dumped-you-for-my-ex hurdle."

"I did, too…back when I assured myself that it wasn't as if I would be seeing you every day."

"I don't remember the word *blunt* being used in reference to you."

"I'm not being insensitive, I'm being real-time honest. Jeez, I wish I had that wine right now."

Chuckling, Derek replied, "Evie, come on, the way we're going I'd better wish you a happy Valentine's, Halloween and Christmas, because it'll be next New Year's before we're apt to run into each other again!"

She moaned with dismay. "Don't call me that."

"What? Evie?" Now he was at a loss for words. He'd meant it as an endearment. For this bizarrely intriguing conversation they were having, Eve seemed too formal, and Evie spoke to his wish that they could still be back in that sunroom with her gently murmuring lyrics that he found himself yearning in that moment to be true.

"It's what my family calls me, especially when they're about to patronize me for something I did or advice I wouldn't take. Another gift that comes with being the youngest. Remember I mentioned my older brother is Nicholas? No one has called him Nick in years. He's a cardiac surgeon. My older sister Sela is a corporate attorney. Her look will give you a freezer burn if you call her anything else."

"I'm not patronizing you, and I understand now how pulling in here the way I did must have panicked you, but—" he gestured to their respective residences "—this is what it is."

She shook her head as if still fighting reality with herself. After a few more seconds, though, she said, "You're taking it awfully well."

"Maybe because I'm honestly glad to see you again." Leaning over a few inches he said, "This is where you could say something like, 'You know what, Derek? I'm happy to have had a chance to see you again, too.'"

With a sheepish smile, she said, "Consider it said."

Continuing to gauge the proximity of their buildings, Derek added, "It *is* odd that we haven't crossed paths sooner."

"The truth is that I rarely see anyone in this place except for service people and the groundskeepers. So many of the residents are professionals who tend to head to their workplaces from five-thirty to seven-thirty every morning. Rae and I usually don't get into our office until nine because we're often on the job later into the evening."

"That would explain it," Derek said, having come to the same conclusion himself. "I'm usually heading in by seven. Although that doesn't explain weekends. What do you do on weekends, play Sleeping Beauty?" That would account for her whipped-cream complexion. His fingers itched to touch her again—in places that would probably leave her with a permanent blush.

"Hardly. That's when I *am* likely to be gone

before daylight, possibly not to return until dark again. We have a number of clients who, out of necessity, schedule their events for the weekend."

"Makes sense."

Derek hoped she would continue, to share what some of those events were like. Despite her reserve, tonight felt a little too close to kismet or destiny to see it end yet. Instead, she opened her door.

As she exited the SUV, he did, too, hurrying to help her, which proved a necessary thing when he saw that she had more ice and snow on her side than he'd previously realized—another indication that the woman had gotten to him in more ways than one. He literally lifted her by her waist as though she were a doll and placed her safety on the clear and dry walkway. "Sorry for not seeing that."

"It's okay," she said a little breathless.

"Derek…I hope you know that I do wish you only happiness?"

She was truly adorable with her big blue eyes refreshingly absent of guile and her mermaid-sleek body half hidden from him by a jacket, whose color perfectly matched her lip gloss. Those lips stirred hunger anew in him. Derek suspected that she didn't have a clue as to how delectable she was because Wes the Weasel had taken her for granted, if not outright neglected her. The betrayal and divorce were the final blows to her crippled self-esteem. He hoped one day Eve would heal enough to believe that she was a delight and would be very easy to fall in love with.

"I wish you the same," he replied with quiet earnestness. They began walking up the sidewalk that bisected their front lawns. "If things were different…"

He waited to see if she would take the bait. Women were supposed to be the curious sex and ask, "What if they were?" But she didn't. She was proving to be an anomaly in more ways than one.

"If things were different," he said again, determined that she hear this anyway. "I would ask you out sometime."

At the crossroads to their respective buildings, she stopped. "That's one of the nicest bad ideas anyone has said to me," she said.

Unsure whether to laugh or curse, Derek had to ask the obvious. "Bad idea why?"

"Because there's baggage, and then there's our kind."

"'Our kind?'"

"Joint baggage."

She made it sound ominous, like a five-year tax audit, or worse. "We aren't the ones who did anything wrong."

"Which is why if we do run into each other now and then, we can say, 'Hello.'"

"I should hope so." Taken aback, Derek

couldn't decide what was more astonishing, that she wanted to pretend that the too-brief, but wholly romantic interlude they'd shared earlier was easier for her to brush aside than it was for him, or that he was somehow tainted by Sam's behavior? Hindsight being the ugly pill that it was had made him accept that Samantha had always shown the impulses of an alley cat. He supposed it was a combination of his patience and voluntary myopia that had allowed the marriage to last as long as it did. No doubt Eve had engaged in her own survival tactics, but she couldn't still be in love with Wes—or was she so angry she was going to judge all men by her two-timing ex's character flaws?

With a sigh, Derek gestured toward her apartment. "I'll wait for you to get inside." When she opened her mouth to protest, he held up his hand. "Humor me. Accept that I'm old school and want to see a lady safe and secure for the evening."

"Okay. Thanks. Sorry." She flapped her arms hopelessly. "I'm just no good at this."

"No, you're not."

But he said it with a smile, and she laughed softly, and finally continued her way to her place.

In truth, she was a pain in places he didn't want to think about. He ached to follow her to her door and kiss away what was left of her lipstick. Some competitive or hungry something compelled him to talk her into agreeing to see him tomorrow or the next day for coffee, lunch, or whatever. If she looked over her shoulder, he would do it.

She didn't look back again until she had her door unlocked. Then she waved and locked up, leaving him to grimly stride to his own apartment. After bolting up behind himself, he stood in the nearly dark, too impersonal living room and felt fatigue descend upon him.

"Note to self," he muttered, pulling at his tie. "Let it go…or move."

"This is the winner of the Best Use of Spices float," the female commentator for the Rose Bowl Parade said on the television.

"And I'm going nuts pretending this is what I want to be doing."

Eve put the last of her meager Christmas ornaments into their box before reaching for the remote and turning off the TV. It was a shame considering that she'd enjoyed this ritual for years, but she just couldn't get into watching today. What's more, she'd already transcribed important dates onto her new calendar—birthdays, anniversaries and appointments—and removed the lights in the window and around her front door. The wreath was neatly tucked in a large trash bag in the coat closet, and the tree was about to go back into its box and join it. She was completely caught up, yet the microwave clock in the kitchen read only 10:57 a.m.

All that remained now was to call her family. But she suddenly dreaded it, despite missing them terribly. How was she going to explain last night without mentioning Derek? They'd known about the party, so there was no avoiding the subject. In fact, they'd be expecting a full recap—mostly in the hopes of discerning that she'd met someone "worthy of her" to quote her father. As good as her parents were at reading her moods and state of mind, her siblings were better than card sharks at reading her. That vetoed any idea about using her computer's Skype application.

With the last items in the closet, she reached for her BlackBerry and scrolled down the contact list keying the number for her parents. Maybe she'd bought herself some time and would only get their answering machine. This was close to the time that they'd be heading to the retirement community where her father and maternal grandfather were likely to squeeze in a round of golf while her mother and the rest of her grandparents discussed who had been wearing the least last night on the evening TV specials. Then they would all head back to the house to wait for the arrival of her siblings, nieces and nephews.

"Eve! Happy New Year, dearest! How was your night?"

Just dive in, Eve thought. "Fine, Mom. Ho-ho to you and Dad. Everything okay down there?"

"Lovely. It's sixty-two degrees, sparkling sunshine and we're about to head out the door."

"Okay, I won't keep you. Give the Grands my love."

"We can talk a minute. But you should call back in the afternoon and visit with everyone else. Your brother and sister say that you've been avoiding them."

"They have busier schedules than I do. It's hard to synchronize a good time to call."

"That's true enough, but they are worried about you, as are the rest of us. Now how was the party? Did you meet anyone interesting?"

"Tons of people," Eve assured her. "The D.A., our congressman, the lady who hosts our local morning talk show up here…"

"Any noteworthy bachelors?"

"A sheik-in-training—some big oil guy's nephew. But he came with a Playboy bunny," she drawled, "and my humble little B-cup chest can't compete with that."

"I'm going to assume you're teasing me the way you always do to stop me from prying." Her mother paused to talk to someone in the background. "Your father sends his love and wants to know when you're coming down for a visit. We discussed your situation over

Christmas dinner, and your sister and brother want you to reconsider letting them arrange for some introductions."

Eve could just imagine. She'd deferred the subject last time by simply telling them she wasn't ready. The second time she pointed out that she would need a Bachelors and Masters to understand half of what their coworkers and friends were talking about. "I'm not exactly where I can talk, Mom. We'll see, okay?"

"Oh, I didn't realize you were still working. Of course, dear. But what will you do after you've finished up there? Are you getting together with friends? I so hope you're not spending the rest of the day sitting in that tiny, dark apartment by yourself."

Eve cringed as she glanced around her spick and span, almost empty and *dark* apartment. "Who, me? No way. There's a skiing party at one of the lodges. I'll grab a hot toddy and strike a sexy pose at the fireplace, until the risk takers get frostbite and rejoin me."

"That sounds more like it. Do watch that no one slips something into your drink. I saw on the news last week—"

"Here's my boss, Mom. Gotta go. Love you."

As soon as she disconnected, Eve grimaced for having deceived her mother, but she simply didn't want to worry her family. What was the point of putting hundreds of miles between herself and them if she wasn't going to finally be independent and be responsible for her own decisions and actions?

She put down the phone and went to peer through the mini blinds. As usual, she saw no one out there, and Derek's black SUV was still parked in the lot, but his mini blinds were shut tight. Lucky him if he was still asleep, she thought with envy. Lucky him if he had *any* sleep.

"And you actually thought you might be preoccupying his mind the way he is yours," she muttered to herself in disgust.

The quiet surroundings did give her the perfect opportunity to get her trash to the Dumpster. She quickly slipped her parka over her oversize, black, V-necked sweater and jeans, grabbed her stuffed trash bag and made her way to the far corner of the property. Although the parking lot was two-thirds full, she didn't see anyone or hear anything, except for the minimal traffic on the two streets that bordered their complex. With the sun shining at full force, the snow sparkled and stung her eyes, making her wish she'd thought to don sunglasses before venturing outside.

After flinging her offering up into the steel bin, she began to retrace her steps. Then she heard a sound that had her glancing up from her diligent navigation of slush piles and puddles. Derek was emerging from his apartment and locking his door.

"Really?" she asked, with a look toward the heavens.

There was no doubt that he would spot her—unless she ducked behind one of the bigger SUVs or pickup trucks. She was feeling very much the coward this morning, but she wasn't that far gone. Besides, with her luck, someone in another apartment was likely to emerge and ask her what she thought she was doing?

Hoping that Derek was preoccupied and wouldn't look her way, she pulled her hood over her head, tucked her hands into her pockets and kept her head down, once again focusing on where she stepped. She was halfway home when she came to the conclusion that he wouldn't remember her jacket from last night. Men didn't pay attention to women's clothing, unless it was skin tight or fastened by string.

"Good morning!"

What part of FBI agent *don't you get, Easton? He's not Wes who, if he wasn't wear-*

ing his contacts, could pass you in your own house and not see you.

Eve stopped and pushed back her hood to find that he'd circled the side way and was almost upon her. He'd remembered his sunglasses and they gave him an air of mystery.

"Hi," Derek said, coming to a halt not two feet away. He slid his glasses up onto his head.

"Hey." She immediately cleared her throat because she sounded like she'd been sucking helium out of a balloon.

"Getting rid of some evidence I should know about?"

He posed the question with mock sternness, but as he nodded toward the Dumpster, she saw the smile in his eyes, even though he was squinting. He was dressed in jeans, a russet suede shirt and a black leather bomber jacket that made him every bit as appealing as he'd been in his business suit last night. Despite having wanted to avoid further contact with him, Eve couldn't deny that he triggered inner turmoil within her, and she was glad that he was in a playful mood.

"What's left of my counterfeiting operation," she countered, pretending pride in her crime. "What I couldn't sell online. Don't bother looking for prints. I wiped everything clean before I bagged it."

"Damn. There goes my hopes for making an arrest and getting to frisk you."

"But we'll always have last night." As soon as the words were out, Eve regretted them. She hadn't meant to send him the wrong signal, he just made it too tempting to play along. "Nice jacket," she added quickly. "It looks vintage."

He inclined his head in thanks. "It is. My father had his grandfather's bomber jacket and I always admired it. Sadly, it didn't hold up well. I found this one on craigslist and couldn't resist."

"You had flyers in your family?"

"Navy, yes."

"Do you fly?"

"No, the bug bypassed me. I try to keep both feet on the ground—or in the water if the opportunity comes up." His expression turned quizzical. "I thought you'd be long gone back up the mountain to resume help with the cleanup?"

Eve shook her head. She wasn't about to make herself available to Rae for another interrogation, no matter how conscientious she was to help out. "But you're obviously off to somewhere. Don't let me keep you."

"Poker with some cronies," he said, with a shrug. "I've reached my saturation point for reading reports and catching up on paperwork."

Eve felt a wave of nostalgia and envy. "That's what my family will do after dinner. Well, cards and dominoes. My grandparents insisted that even we kids learn. It guaranteed that they'd never run short of players."

"I'll bet you're pretty good—except at the poker face."

Wrinkling her nose, she admitted, "You'll be astonished to learn that you're not the first person to have said that."

"I'd invite you to come along, but it's stag. I wouldn't subject your tender ears to that."

"I'm sure I'm no match to you high rollers anyway." She took a step to signal her retreat, only to remember something. "D.A. Maines— is he okay? His house?"

"Fine. Perfect. The neighbor's place has damage, but it's limited to two rooms." Derek's gaze grew concerned. "Are you catching a cold? Your voice sounds different and your nose is getting pinker by the second."

She should never have mentioned her family; the tears she'd been fighting after calling home were threatening again. "Probably allergies from the dust while taking down Christmas stuff. But just in case, I better keep my distance and not contaminate you." She took another backward step. "Good luck."

"Take care of *you*."

Eve waved her appreciation for his concern and cut a brisk about-face to increase her pace back to her apartment. Her mood sank with each step as she processed what he'd told her.

He had friends, a life, things to do. How silly and egotistical to hide indoors believing he'd been lying in wait for her!

Note to self—he's out of your league! Get back to doing what you came up here to do.

Chapter Three

"Eve! Will you come in here please?"

Rae had only been in the office a few minutes before that sharp command came. It sent the other five people in the outer room trying to hide behind their laptops. Sitting at a desk that faced the others in their lobby office, Eve gave up on the call she'd been repeatedly attempting without success since arriving two hours ago. A consistent busy signal at a florist the day after New Year's was an attention-getter. It should be their quiet time, so either someone big had died, or there had been a number of passings over the holiday.

"On my way," she called back. Wryly noting the other ladies' reactions, she grabbed her notebook and daily planner, and hurried into Rae's resplendent copper-and-leopard-skin-wallpapered office and closed the door behind her. "The troops want to know if you need sweetener in your coffee?"

"I'm not being witchy, I'm legitimately upset. Where are the brochures for the historical building fundraiser that were promised first thing this morning? I was going to take some to the luncheon—a good idea, *n'est-ce pas?* And who decided *mud* brown napkins were a good color for a formal event?" She pushed the offending item across her desk with her pen as though afraid the color would come off and stain her designer winter-white suit.

Eve recognized the napkin and realized that was a possibility. *"Oui, il est si,"* she replied obediently, knowing Rae's penchant for constant self-improvement. But she had the French, *Is it not so? Yes, it is so* down pat. What she wanted was for something to go smoothly this morning. They were starting January seriously behind. "Lisa expedited the brochures the minute she arrived. We know they're on the freight carrier's truck for delivery today. The time is anyone's guess. I knew Honor had put a report on your desk, but I didn't realize she'd put a napkin in there, too. I'm guessing that since The Garden Show does include dirt, she thought the City of Denver booth should use a color that was a thematic match. I'm sure when she found that big box of them in the storage room, she also thought she was doing you a huge favor and saving the firm money." The city planned on serving herbal tea to visitors at the February show, as they handed out maps of the city's parks.

"I should have known this was Honor's

doing." Dropping her pen on her desk, Rae rested her head in her hand and used the opportunity to peek under her fingers at their newest employee sitting closest to the entryway. "The poor dear. She makes a fine receptionist, but there's no future for her on our front line."

While Eve ultimately agreed, she couldn't blame the middle-aged widow entirely for what had happened. "We really should have eaten the loss and tossed the napkins the first time we realized the color bled the moment the napkin gets wet. It's not like we were going to risk using them for another client's event."

Looking ready to justify her decision, Rae opened her mouth to respond, only to check herself. "Fudge," she muttered instead. Dropping the napkin into her trash can under her desk, she said, "Have her call Carlos down in Maintenance to get him to take those things to the Dumpster. Then add white cocktail napkins to your list. You're still handling the nonperishable shopping this afternoon for the Medical Center open house, aren't you?"

That had been the plan when they last went over schedules before the holiday. "I have so many fires to put out, I can't afford to lose the time here. If you don't mind, I'll do it on my way home this evening?"

"As busy a week as it's going to be, I hate for you to have to do that, but thank you. What else is wrong?"

"I can't get anyone to answer at Executive Floral Services. Did some big deal in Denver die that I don't know about?" she asked her boss. She'd accused Rae of sleeping with a radio scanner beside the bed, since she was always on top of the news in town.

"No, but there was some cable cut at a construction site by the airport. That could have something to do with the problem." Rae browsed through the other paperwork and mail that was covering her desk. "Why don't you detour that way on your lunch hour?"

"Because I'm not taking lunch, for the same reason I'm not going shopping for those supplies until later." Realizing Rae hadn't noticed yet, Eve updated her. "At any moment Kristen is going to admit that she's come down with the flu and—"

"Good grief, where's my disinfectant spray?" Rae opened her top desk drawer and took out a bottle of hand sanitizer instead. "Now the alcohol in this will make me look like a crone. Tell her to get out. Now. We can't afford to spread her condition through the office. And tell her to stop and get a case of chicken soup on the way home—I'll reimburse her."

Smiling at her boss's logic, as well as her generosity, in the face of her germ phobia, she stepped out to have a few words with Kristen Minnow, then returned. "She says you're the nicest scary person she knows."

"Liar, that's pure you," Rae said as she waved at the departing woman through her window. As Eve resumed her seat, Rae sighed. "I'm sorry for being so tightly wound. I'd push up my sleeves and help you with things, but I have that Chamber of Commerce luncheon."

"Yeah, that would be a smart one not to miss considering you're an honoree. We don't have a job if you aren't out there doing yours. Fabulous suit, by the way."

Turning up the collar, Rae relaxed enough to preen. "Thank you kindly. You don't think it's too Good Witch? I know some there will be thinking a black pointed hat would be more appropriate."

"Only your competitors." Crossing her arms over her sapphire-blue tunic sweater-skirt set, Eve said, "You look regal as well as radiant. Wasn't that the idea?"

Shaking her glossy red coif, a move that also made her gold-and-diamond earrings sparkle in the light, Rae sighed with satisfaction. "You're so good for my ego, and the best business decision I ever made."

Eve wasn't convinced that she agreed, considering that four of the five people left working in the next room had degrees, pedigrees and ambitions that made her look like an underachiever.

"Well, your investment is in danger of heading for a hospital, as well. I don't understand how so many businesses are bellying up, but we're expanding. The problem is that Angie will be shortly gone on maternity leave, and you can count Kristen out for this week. That leaves Margaret, Lisa, Tara and me as your experienced staff. If I can't whip Honor into some sort of shape by Thursday, you're going to have to help out at the fundraiser Friday night, and I don't mean just taking bows and schmoozing with potential clients."

"Your point is well taken. Any new calls that

come in for this month or next, don't promise a 'can do,' until we review our calendar closely." Rae put away the little bottle and studied Eve more closely. "Is something else going on with you besides the workload? You look almost bluer than that becoming outfit."

Eve knew better than to voice what was really on her mind. Besides, Rae deserved better from her having just reminded her that they were buried in work. "I'm fine. Just worried that we won't get it all done on time."

"You never told me how you spent the rest of your New Year's. Did Mr. S.A.C. ask you out?"

"Who's Mr.— Oh. Do you know the number of people in his office?" Eve asked, remembering that not-so-small detail. "He's practically a king."

"Gus said more like a god."

Eve was glad she was sitting down. It was even more intimidating than she thought.

"So did he?" At Eve's numb look, Rae asked in pedantic fashion, "Did-he-ask-you-out?"

"No."

The quick reply had Rae smirking. "I don't believe you. Where does he live? Was it far to his place?"

The incredulousness of it all got the best of Eve. "Actually, I could walk there."

"Do tell? Did you happen to share that little fact? Heaven knows, Derek has ambition if he's already achieved the position he has at his age, but relationship-wise men can be like lunkers, they're slow to respond, until something delectable drops in front of their noses."

"How romantic to be compared to fish bait."

"I was describing a type of male lethargy."

"I'm familiar with the species. I married one of them." Ignoring Rae's look of sympathy, Eve added, "At any rate, there was no need to explain anything about our residences. How would you have said it? *Tout ce que j'avais a faire ne tait point.*"

"All you had to do was point?" Rae repeated slowly. Then she got excited. "Do you mean he's in the complex next to yours?"

"Not even that far. The *building* facing mine. In decent weather, we could slide open our windows and converse like our great-grand-mothers might have in inner cities while hanging the wash."

Rae threw her head back and laughed with gusto. "That's too good to be true."

"Easy for you to say."

"How on earth have you managed not to meet before the other night?" Rae wondered aloud.

"From what we gathered, our schedules are just off enough to allow us to miss each other."

"Fascinating." Rae studied her as though every word out of her mouth were the diamonds and pearls of the old *Rose Red, Rose*

White children's fairy tale. "Considering the salary he has to be getting, I wonder why he didn't invest in a house? Nice as your apartments are, it's still money being thrown away. The mortgage interest deduction would have been a plus, too."

Maybe, like her, he wasn't certain how long he would be staying, Eve thought. But to Rae she simply shrugged. "He probably knew how busy he would be and didn't want that much more responsibility."

"That's true." Rae couldn't—or wouldn't—hide her pleasure. "But he *did* ask you out, didn't he?"

"I have to get back to my desk," Eve said, collecting her things and rising. But one look at Rae's steady stare and she confessed, "I told him that it wasn't a good idea."

That clearly wasn't what Rae wanted to hear. "Have you lost your mind? You had on *the* dress of the evening, the man was visibly mesmerized…you even kissed him! Then you decided to put up roadblocks?"

"They're serious ones," Eve said more quietly, hoping Rae would take the hint and not broadcast their conversation to the office at large. "We have too much baggage between us."

"Toss it. You're both free and you know what the other has gone through. You can skip the walking-on-eggshells stage that others have to deal with," Rae said warming to her subject. "Best of all, you'll never run out of things to talk about. You have each of your ex's bad habits and missteps to discuss."

"That's not funny, or healthy." Then Eve thought of another downer. "I don't think I want to kiss a man who ends up comparing me to the woman who stole *my* husband."

"Darling," Rae replied, "you already have— and he's smitten. I saw it with my own twenty-twenty's."

Eve had had plenty of time to mentally sabotage that notion. "That illusion wasn't me. This is who I am—makeup half worn off and it isn't even noon." She leaned closer to remind Rae, "All I could wear under that dress were modesty petals and a thong!"

"I'd never seen you look better." Rae checked her watch and sighed. "This conversation isn't over, but I have to go, otherwise I'll be late." As Rae reached for her purse, she added, "I won't be back this afternoon, so when you get the proposal for the Franklin event finished, fax it to me at the house. If Elliot Franklin happens to call, tell him that I'll get back to him later this afternoon. I'm heading straight home to get ready for Gus's dinner party with his new clients tomorrow night."

The Franklin estimate! As Rae left the office, Eve's heart plummeted. What with everything else going on this morning, she'd forgotten all about the retirement party for the senior partner of *Franklin & Franklin.* Of all the blunders…the requested gala for the prestigious firm would be one of their most profitable events of the season.

"Enough daydreaming about Derek and what-ifs," she told herself. Returning to her desk, she dug for the folder that barely contained more than Rae's recommendations.

"Is there anything I can do, Eve?" Honor asked, approaching her desk. "I know Mrs. Grainger was mad at me for the napkins. I saw her through the window."

Despite her own worries, Eve managed a reassuring smile. She liked the pleasant woman, who was trying to rejoin the workforce after seventeen years as a stay-at-home mom. At least Honor didn't act as socially elite as the younger members of the staff sometimes did. "Saving the company money is always a worthy idea, Honor. But they're inferior material. It's not entirely your fault, though. We should have disposed of the box sooner." She asked her to call downstairs as Rae directed. "Why don't you go on to lunch after that? When you get back I'll have a list of calls I'd like you to make for me."

"Can I bring you something back?"

"That would be great." She quickly reached into her bag for a twenty-dollar bill. "Just get me whatever you're having. This should cover both."

And so went the week. By Thursday evening, as Eve headed toward her apartment complex, it was well past eight o'clock. She couldn't wait to peel off her stiletto-heeled boots, strip and step under the hot spray of her shower, after which she intended on dropping into bed, even though she'd had little lunch and no dinner. She would have skipped the shower, too, but while she'd succeeded in getting caught up at the office, she was as tight as a bungee cord tied to a speed train.

But as she approached her apartment complex, she saw something that instantaneously snapped her out of her fatigue. Making a split-second decision, she continued past her driveway entrance. It was Derek again. He'd pulled in just ahead of her.

"How crazy is that?" she said to the pickup truck ahead of her.

Three out of four days this week, she'd come in either just before or after him. After all these months of missing each other, it seemed fate was now changing course and making it nearly impossible not to run into each other. To avoid that, she once pretended a quick phone call and had waved to him and pulled out, leaving to keep from having to speak with him. The next time, she'd slowed to a crawl until he'd entered his apartment. Certain that her luck couldn't hold, accelerating and driving around the block seemed to be her best option this time.

Once she returned and did park, she quickly took her mail at the island of boxes beside his building. Not even bothering to look at what was there, she walked crisply along the sidewalk, her heels creating a sharp staccato sound in the January night. Thank goodness it was an adults-only complex. Except for road traffic, it was such a peaceful place. Perfect sleeping conditions, she thought, letting herself into her apartment.

She sighed with relief when she locked up after herself. But as she dropped her purse and mail on the kitchen counter, there was a knock on the front door.

What on earth...?

Retracing her steps, she peeked out the security hole, only to cover the tiny circlet with her hand. *You thought yourself entirely too clever.*

Wishing she had the courage—or gall—to

ignore him, she opened the door to guiltily meet Derek's mild look. He stood there like her—jacket still on—with a measuring cup dangling off of his left index finger.

"Are you serious about going through so much trouble to avoid me?"

He asked the question as though pondering one of life's confusing mysteries. So much for holding out any hope that he really had come to borrow sugar, milk or quarters for his next poker game. Giving him his due, she supposed he'd been on to her since New Year's Day.

"I didn't want you to think that contrary to what I said, I was trying to get your attention," she told him.

"Evie," he began drolly, "a direct meteor hit couldn't be as explicit as you were…but it would take that to forget that you're on this planet. You're starting to give me a complex, you know. That's not good for a guy in my line of work."

Eve couldn't help but smile at the way he was trying to make himself look like a forlorn pup—and failing badly. "Well, who needs that on her conscience?"

"Better," he said. "We're practically in detente." He gestured over his shoulder toward the open-air shopping center across the boulevard from them, specifically at the cozy bistro at the end closest to them. "I need food, definitely something more restorative than a nuked dinner. You want to discuss psychological disarmament over there?"

He was smooth and disarming, and he almost made her forget what an important and powerful man he was. But not quite. "Derek, I've had these S&M boots on for over twelve hours, and my brain has been worked still harder. I wouldn't be good company. All I really wanted was a steaming-hot shower and bed."

Although he eyed the boots *and* her black

leather slacks with greater respect, he didn't let up. "A glass of wine before bed would do you a world of good. It's not a date," he insisted before she could protest further. He laid his hand against his chest. "I'd be pleased if you'd be my guest—sue me, I'm old-fashioned—but if that makes you uncomfortable, I'll risk making my southern ancestors roll in their graves and ask for separate checks."

The wine did sound appealing, and she would be foolish not to have a bite herself. Most of all, though, she was finding it impossible to resist the appeal in his eyes. "Let me change out of these boots," she told him, "or I won't make it across the street."

Not five minutes later, now in moccasin-style ankle boots, Eve accompanied Derek into The Corner Grill, a salmon-painted brick and lead-glass establishment that was two-thirds eclectic restaurant and one-third bar, where currently regulars were roosting to watch whatever game was keeping things lively.

They were promptly led to a cozy booth by a window that looked out toward their complex. But what enhanced the view were the tiny LED lights covering the shrubs and trees. A flameless candle on the table added to the touch of romance.

"I'm Billie," their petite, ponytailed waitress told them. "What can I get you to drink?"

Having removed his all-weather coat, Derek slid onto the opposite bench and gestured invitingly to Eve as he said, "I'd like a glass of the house cabernet, and the lady will have…"

"That sounds perfect," Eve told her.

They begged off on immediately accepting the day's special appetizer, and chose to peruse the menus instead. Billie left them to fill their drink order.

"Maybe we should have ordered a bottle," Derek said, once they were alone.

"Not unless you're ready to watch me slide off this bench and under the table. I meant it about it being a tough week, and tomorrow night we have an event, so I'll be nursing that one glass." Eve glanced around. It had been a while since she'd last come here. She didn't like going out alone and this atmosphere with its dark-toned wood and low lighting induced intimacy. "I do like it here, though. I'd forgotten how pretty it is."

After murmuring his agreement, Derek admitted, "I tend to eat at the bar. There's always a game on the TV, so conversation can be kept to a minimum without seeming blatantly rude."

"Poor G-man. Most guys would enjoy being relentlessly hit upon."

He gave her the semblance of a narrow-eyed look of warning. "I wasn't bragging. There are guys who can't resist looking for a buddy to cheer on their team with."

"And maybe finance the next round of drinks."

"You catch on fast, grasshopper."

"I was intimidated by the bar the one time I came alone," Eve admitted. "I opted for a table and then had to pretend that I didn't notice how everyone was having a better time than I was." When they weren't giving her pitying or curious looks.

"I have to ask," Derek said, drawing her back to the present. "Why aren't you already wearing a huge rock and planning a six-figure wedding?"

Aghast, Eve blinked at him as though he'd just asked her if she had ever been tempted to dye her hair green? "My parents are financially comfortable, but it's their hard-earned money, not mine or my siblings'. We were raised with a healthy dose of common sense. Reckless spending for what doesn't improve,

and can change the future of a union is ridiculous."

"And yet you're an events planner."

"Assistant to an events planner."

"What I was trying to find out," Derek continued with gentle doggedness, "is why you're
not in a serious relationship yet? Please don't
tell me that you didn't mean it about not pining
for your ex, or that you're hoping that, having
realized his mistake, he'll come after you?"

"Good grief, no way!" Eve wouldn't want
Wes back even if he wasn't an expectant father. "I'm offended and bruised, not a door-
mat despite how things may have seemed to
you and Sam."

"I thought no such thing," Derek replied gently.

Somewhat mollified, Eve shrugged.
"Statistically, I'm in the category that says di-
nosaurs will emerge from melting polar ice
caps before I'm likely to marry again. Men my

age are still hoping a Denver Broncos cheer-
leader will drop into their laps, while men
your age are starting to look for trophy wives.
I don't have enough zeroes in my financial
statement."

"For a pretty woman, you're such a cynic."

"I am?" Amused, Eve snapped her fingers.
"I overshot my goal. I was aiming for realist."

Billie returned with their wine, which forced
them to pay more attention to the menus.
Derek insisted on ordering a small sampler
plate for them to share, and then Eve asked
for the salmon, while he decided on the rib
eye steak for himself. He wanted to wait on
the salad to have it with his meal, while she
stayed with grilled vegetables and rice that
came with her dinner.

Alone again, Derek reached for his glass.
"Thank you for saving me from my microwave." He touched his glass to hers.

"Back at you. I'm sorry that you've had a tough week, too."

"No more shop talk tonight. That's what put us in this condition."

Eve admitted that he had a point. "But then what does that leave me with except to ask how the poker game went on Sunday?"

This time Derek looked embarrassed. "There's another subject that should probably be avoided."

"Oh, dear. You lost?"

"You ruined my concentration. Are you feeling guilty? I usually eat a week's worth of lunches on my winnings."

"What did I do except try not to hold you up?"

"You made me think of your blue eyes, and Etta James and that there was a better place to be than a cigar-smoke-filled room."

Eve's answering look held mild reproach. But when she saw him unable to resist tugging at his burgundy and silver tie, she relented. "I changed out of my killer boots. Take off the tie before you strangle yourself."

"Bless you," he muttered, doing just that. Then he opened the top two buttons of his shirt. As he stuffed the tie into his jacket pocket, he said, "One good turn deserves another. You've been trying to hide that you're turning your head from side to side to work the kinks out of your neck." He slid out of his seat and ordered, "Slide over." Once she did, albeit reluctantly, he settled beside her and immediately began to massage her shoulders, then her neck. "I can feel you're all knots even through this suede jacket."

Intending to assure him that she was fine and point out that people were noticing them, instead she gasped and murmured her appreciation of his sensitive ministrations, which were almost instantly effective. "Oh...that is beyond wonderful."

"If you slip off the jacket, I can do better."

"I'm okay."

"You can't still be cold?"

Reluctantly, Eve shrugged out of the black suede jacket. Derek helped, and then went back to massaging her.

"No wonder you didn't want to take it off. Great sweater. What is that material, cashmere?" he asked, as he worked.

Eve knew the sweater delineated her figure as much as her New Year's dress had, and could feel her cheeks heat under his scrutiny. "You're incorrigible."

"You're softer than a bunny."

Accepting that it was useless to ask him not to inundate her with compliments, she acknowledged, "It is sumptuous. This is the only reason I like cold weather, cashmere sweaters and scarves. Ow!" She stiffened as he came upon one particularly painful spot on her neck.

"Sorry." He planted a light kiss at her nape.

"Derek—"

"Do you have one of those bean bag things that you can heat in the microwave and place around your neck? That would help you when you head for bed tonight."

"Come to think of it, I do. Thanks for the reminder."

Derek was extra careful with her after that. Eve could have moaned out loud, it felt so good, but she began feeling self-conscious at the looks they were attracting from around the room. "Um…I think I'm much better now, thanks."

With a resigned sigh, he switched back to his side of the booth. "I can enjoy your blush better from this vantage point anyway."

Watching the gray tones of his eyes change and some satisfied emotion lighten them, Eve felt hopelessly lost. "I never saw one hint of this in your personality back in Texas."

"Of course not. But things are different now.

You're the one who's trying to stay committed to a conduct that no longer applies."

"'Committed...?'"

As Billie arrived with the sampler platter, Eve sat there taken aback by his pronouncement. However, she realized that he was right—at least somewhat. When was it going to sink in that Wes didn't get to critique everything and weigh how it affected *his* work and interests? But how did one change without feeling like she was losing her entire identity? Conscientious and careful was who she'd been—wife of Coach Prescott. Stalwart Booster Club and PTA volunteer taking on whatever extracurricular job that would help Wes shine in his position.

With Billie departing, Derek said, "Allow me," and picked up the small saucer that the waitress had set before her. Using his fork, he placed an egg roll and fried shrimp on her plate.

When he reached for a buffalo wing, she stopped him. "I'll pass on those if you don't mind. My stomach doesn't handle the sauce well, and I don't want to risk dropping one on my sweater. I can be as messy as a two-year-old with finger food."

"Are you? We'll have to try ribs sometime. It would be worth paying your dry cleaning bill to see you with barbecue sauce on your chin and nose." When she only gave him a slow look from under her lashes, Derek complained, "Do you know I think I saw you actually laugh twice in all the time we lived next to each other?"

Countering, Eve replied, "I didn't see you laugh *ever*. And for the record, I smiled almost all the time. After all, I was the ambassador to the Kingdom of Wes!"

Derek's brief laugh held disdain. "Yeah, I noticed that. I said *laugh*. The first time was when the neighbor's obnoxious standard poodle escaped and knocked you down as you were watering your flowers."

"Aw," Eve murmured, remembering. "Elvis was attention deprived. When he wasn't locked inside, he was confined to their yard with that privacy fence that tortured the poor brute. He had sounds and smells, but no sight except for what he could glimpse between slats and the wood knotholes that he tried to dig out with his teeth and trimmed nails. Why people who work all day think they need something so social as a dog, I don't know."

"I was envious as he licked water off you." Not missing a beat, Derek continued. "And then when it snowed and sleeted, then snowed some more, you were checking on our elderly neighbors and getting their paper and mail. You landed on your butt at least three times before making it back to your yard, where you gave up and made a snow angel where you last dropped."

Wholly suspicious, Eve said, "You couldn't have been home that much. Sam must have witnessed all that and told you."

Derek scoffed at the idea. "You didn't know Samantha. She would have told 25 percent of the story—namely your stumbles, and she would have labeled your warmhearted gestures as goody-two-shoes behavior, but she would have managed to leave out anything that made you look compassionate, let alone lovely."

Despite the compliment, Eve remained defensive. "Well, I laughed plenty of times." Thinking back to that experience, she grew wistful. "I thought about asking the Millers if I could dog-sit for Elvis, but Wes was allergic."

"I'll bet."

"Prejudicial, Special Agent-in-Charge."

"Sue me, *Ms.* Easton." His expression was all mellowness as he took another sip of wine. "I thought the town was going to bronze your

Yard-of-the-Month sign and cement it in place. I never saw Wes help you. Let me guess—he's allergic to grass, too?"

He must have thought her a fool for trying to make a place of serenity and relaxation for them—even after Wes declared that he was outside most of the day and in the evening he wanted his air-conditioning or heater, depending on the season. "He worked, so I felt I should take care of the property. Besides, I loved being outdoors," she said quietly. "I didn't mind."

With a murmur of regret, Derek wiped his hands in his napkin, only to reach over to cover her hand with his. "I know you didn't. I never saw so many flowers outside of a nursery or florist. Forgive me, I guess I'm still smarting a little over Sam's lack of appreciation and support. You'll remember Sam's helping hand consisted of the two ferns I'd buy yearly for the front porch. Inevitably, I'd need to go to

Quantico or elsewhere, and by the time I got home, I could guarantee she'd have managed to kill them."

While Eve had no reason to champion Samantha, she felt the need to be fair. "I was only in your house a handful of times, but I did notice that Sam was a meticulous house-keeper."

"You're being polite. Admit it—you thought you'd walked into the final hours of an estate sale?"

Eve couldn't help but cover her face with one hand to keep from choking on the bite of shrimp she'd just ingested. "Okay," she wheezed, "so her idea of decorating was a lit-tle minimalistic."

"Interesting how she didn't carry that style to adorning herself."

"To each their own." Taking a necessary sip of wine, Eve had to admit the woman had exhibited her share of bling. She'd believed they were all gifts from Derek. That's what Sam would insinuate. "I didn't realize that you minded."

"I minded most when a new credit card bill materialized where we'd never had an account before." Shrugging, Derek added, "But then, I was extremely dedicated to my work, gone a great deal and I knew she was increasingly bored, so maybe I'm not entirely blameless. Unlike you, Sam wasn't a joiner and, like you, she didn't have to work if she didn't want to. Trust me when I say she didn't want to. Inevitably, we grew apart. I admit that I noticed and did nothing about it." His look grew pensive. "I would understand if you blamed me as much as Sam for breaking up your marriage."

She couldn't be that dishonest. He'd already said more than she deserved to know considering this was just a dinner, not group therapy, and she believed in the theory that someone couldn't steal a heart that wasn't ready to be taken. "Marriage isn't easy," she murmured.

"It should be." Meeting her surprised look, Derek shrugged. "Easier anyway. It's a partnership. Two souls on a journey. Respect. Passion. Love. I thought *you* had it."

So did she…for the first two or three years anyway. "Had you fooled, didn't I?"

"I want it." He seemed to catch the intensity in his own voice and retreated into himself. "Maybe next time."

Was he literally dropping a gigantic hint? No, she insisted to herself. Neighbors and former neighbors or not, they were still 90 percent strangers. He was simply doing what men do—or what she'd heard from listening to the women in the office describe their dating and relationship experiences. Guys threw out ideas and hypothesis instead of questions to get a reaction and find out where you stood and what they had to say to make points with you. She had hoped Derek wouldn't be one of those, but hadn't he just described how human he was?

Eve had committed to a different approach since her divorce, as well. Uncompromising honesty. "I hope you find what you're looking for," she said sincerely. "Frankly, this week at work has made me think more and more about returning to Texas."

After a noticeable hesitation and covert look, Derek asked, "I thought you enjoyed your job?"

"I do."

"I know you miss your family, but wouldn't the sudden loss of you impact Rae? From what you've indicated, she's invested a good deal of time and effort into you."

"I know. That's what's holding me back. But my sister's pregnant, did I mention that? Sela is thirty-five, so this is probably her last child. I was in the delivery room when her son Zach was born. Her husband Mitchell was still in

the reserves then and deployed. I cut the um-
bilical cord. It's true what they say about it
creating a lifelong bond. I'm kidding myself
that phone calls and using Skype is enough."

"You just need to take a break and go see
him. Them. This is your first holiday period
away, it's natural to be blue and second-guess
yourself."

"I suppose you're right."

"Are you close with any of the other people
in the office?"

"Ah...no." Eve hadn't expected the question and was still in the midst of resolving
the tricky situation in her own mind. "Aside
from Rae and me, there are five ladies. The
newest is the eldest. Honor was a stay-at-home
mom who's now returning to the workforce for
the sake of her children's educational future.
She's big-hearted, but lacks some abilities Rae
prizes in her staff. Rae is about to reduce her
to being a receptionist and gopher. As for Lisa,

Tara, Kristen and Angie, let's just say they're like the coed Four Horsemen. They're all in their early or mid-twenties, they come from affluent families, they see this job as a step toward either owning their own businesses or networking to marrying up, and there's this not-so-subtle elitism and attitude of entitlement that emanates from them. Angie married last year and is about to start pregnancy leave. That's the other reason that I'm torn about what to do."

"Thank you, Angie," Derek said, openly unrepentant.

"So unfair," Eve replied in a gently reprimanding tone. "It's not like I can question you about your employees."

"I have four *agents* out on maternity leave." When Eve's mouth formed a small O, he nodded. "Yes, and crime—whether it's the straightforward or the complicated international variety—hasn't eased up one iota."

Since Eve couldn't will herself invisible, she began folding the napkin on her lap into a fan. "Why do you even want to listen to me? This event being an exception, so much of what we do is superfluous compared to your work."

"You're refreshing," he replied, without missing a beat. "I've met my share of those young women you're talking about. Hell, I married a form of one—and you know it, although you're too nice to admit as much. What's the event you were talking about for tomorrow?"

Eve wished she could take "refreshing" as a compliment, but she was afraid that what he really meant was that she was more like Honor than she thought. "It's a fundraiser, in this case a worthy cause. The Grandy Building has qualified for Historical Society recognition, but needs help in surviving. Our clients are hoping to somehow make enough repairs to where the university can afford to accept it as the site for their new history department."

"What does that entail for you aside from ordering enough booze and biscuits?"

"I spent ten hours this week exploring the place and talking to the last living Grandy, who has the recall necessary to help me create a tour for our biggest donors. Then I read…I forget how many newspaper and family files on it. The other ladies will be serving refreshments and handing out donation envelopes and pledge cards, while Rae will be collecting them."

"Eve, that's marvelous."

"I don't know about that, but I do enjoy something like this more than a politician's campaign party."

Their main course arrived and yet the conversation still seemed to flow. Eve found herself getting more relaxed as Derek told her a few anecdotes about his experiences with the Bureau. For all of the seriousness of their work, the agents were human beings, and often real characters.

At some point she realized she was on her second glass of wine. Although she strived to ignore it, when Billie came to apologetically announce they were closing the restaurant side of the building, she found the glass almost empty.

"You're welcome to go sit at the bar if you'd like," Billie told them. "They'll be open until one."

Glancing around, Eve realized they were the last two in the dining room. That spoke volumes as to how rapt she'd been in listening to Derek. But studying him as he dealt with the bill, she also realized that he'd been entirely aware of the passage of time. Smooth, she thought, deciding for that reason alone, she wouldn't argue over the check.

Once they stepped outside, she quickly

buttoned her jacket and pulled up the collar. "Thank you for this," she told him.

"My pleasure. It wasn't painful, was it?" As they crossed the boulevard, traffic was light, but Derek still put his arm around her as he gauged the speed and distance of a car that had turned onto the street.

"I never said it would be. Awkward, maybe."

"But it wasn't that, either."

He wasn't asking a question, which pulled another smile from her. "No," she admitted.

They made it across their parking lot and started up the sidewalk toward their buildings talking about the next weather system due early next week. From the lack of lights on in most apartments, it looked like they were almost the last awake in their complex.

"What are you doing Saturday?" Derek asked.

Eve had sensed this was coming, and she still stumbled over her reply. "Oh, I don't think—"

"As tense as you were tonight, you'll be in dire need of some R&R after tomorrow night's event."

They'd come to her door and Eve gripped her keys until they hurt against her palm. "Derek, don't. Tonight was great, but my future is too unsettled. What's the point?"

"Only this."

Before she realized what he intended, he framed her face with his hands and kissed her. His lips were warm but firm on hers and she felt his yearning as the ardent caress seeped through her. It was every bit as potent as those two glasses of wine and made a joke of her determined resistance. In fact, she was about to wrap her arms around him when he released her.

Derek plunged his hands in his pants pockets as though it was the only choice he had short of kissing her again. "Go on, get inside and lock up," he told her gruffly. "I don't want to have to look out my window in ten minutes and find you still standing out here turning into a delectable popsicle."

What really propelled her was his stance; it allowed her to see his badge and more on his service belt. The G-man could flirt with the best of them, and she was too human to deny that she'd been affected. But in the end, she would be a fool not to remember that he was a company man. That meant things that she couldn't consider given her present mind-set.

"'Nite," she murmured, and hurried inside.

After locking up, she laid her forehead against the cool, steel door. "No, no, no," she whispered. He was wonderful, but the wrong man, at the wrong time, in the wrong place.

Chapter Four

The persistent knocking on her front door jarred Eve awake. "Are you kidding me? *Again?*"

Lifting her face out of her pillow, she cast a dazed glance at the clock on the night table that told her that it was barely eight o'clock. Saturday or Sunday? she wondered. She felt groggy enough to have slept through an entire day.

It took several seconds for her to distinguish that the light creeping around the privacy blinds was daylight, not apartment security lights. But regardless of how much sleep she did or didn't get, she wasn't yet ready to face the world, let alone an impatient visitor.

"Go away," she muttered, dropping her head back onto the pillow. Unfortunately, her mind had been jarred enough to crank into gear.

Derek wouldn't be pulling something, would he? He'd known that she would be having a late night yesterday.

As fatigue tried to lure her back to sleep, the sounds of other doors opening and slamming, plus loud voices roused her anew. Now someone was pounding on an inner wall? No, that was knocking at doors several apartments away.

The assault on her door resumed. Something was definitely going on.

"Eve! Wake up!"

"You think anyone can sleep with the racket you're making?" she muttered, forcing herself to sit up. This time she recognized the voice. Muttering under her breath, she shuffled—mostly by memory than focus—through her apartment and, at the front door, peered through the security hole.

"Eve! It's an emergency!"

It was Derek all right, but he wasn't alone. Others were milling around, some zipping by so fast, she couldn't distinguish male, female, clothing or age. *Emergency* began to take on a real connotation, and she turned the deadbolt and opened the door just enough to blink at him and the scene in general. "No fire in here. Thanks for asking."

"There could be if we don't clear the area. Don't you smell it?"

"Smell what?" She sniffed and immediately wished she hadn't. "Ew." But then her mind finally snapped to full alert. "Gas?"

"They think the line leak or break is behind your building, but we're all being told to get out. Now. Drag on some clothes or at least a jacket and let's go."

"I'll be right there."

She was a little slower than that, taking long enough to use the bathroom, run a toothbrush over her teeth, drag on jeans and the first pullover sweater she could grab, which happened to be white and a poor choice, and that was all because Derek was banging on the door again.

Grabbing her shoulder bag and shoving her feet into sneakers, she yanked open the door to Derek and a tense police officer.

"That wasn't fast enough?" she asked in self-defense.

In reply, Derek took hold of her arm and, with long strides that forced her to jog, led her to the parking lot. The officer apparently moved on to other laggards.

"I had to show the officer my ID to keep him from citing you for civil disobedience. Do you not realize what kind of blast we could all be looking at?"

Although the idea of an explosion chilled Eve more than the frigid morning air, she felt the need to explain. "Did he expect me to run into the parking lot in my sleep shirt and socks?"

"He would have loved it. Me, too. But I would have gallantly swept you into my SUV to protect your modesty and keep your delightful extremities from frostbite. Which is basically what we're going to do anyway, because just before you deigned to join us, they told us it might be this evening or tomorrow before we can get back inside."

Eve was appalled. "I haven't washed my face or combed my hair!"

Having reached his vehicle, Derek noted, "I don't know, the half-awake punkish look is kind of cute."

Eve caught a glimpse of her image in the passenger window, and self-consciously hand-combed her short hair into what she hoped was more respectable. For his part, Derek looked wonderful—showered and shaven, his government-short brown hair neatly combed. For pity's sake, she thought, his laundered jeans had a crease, and his black ski jacket with the red band around each arm, looked very *GQ*-worthy over his black pullover sweater. He was even wearing sensible boots for this kind of climate.

"When did you realize this was going on?" she asked, as he opened the passenger door for her.

"About fifteen minutes before things went from troubling to full-fledged evacuation. I'd been up for over an hour before that," he told her, once he settled behind the driver's seat.

Other people were doing the same thing they were, hurrying to their vehicles. Many looked fairly put out with the whole situation, too. More than a few didn't even have a jacket, and one was barefoot. Regardless of Derek's half compliment, Eve lowered the visor and reached into her purse for her makeup bag.

"If you're going to be driving around anyway," she began, "I'd consider it a huge kindness if we could go through a drive-through for some coffee."

"I was about to suggest it. I've already had my share, but what's your preference? The calories with coffee in it, or the industrial-strength stuff?"

"Industrial strength, please. Skip any sweetener."

"How about a biscuit or croissant?"

"Not yet. Thanks."

Derek navigated the turns and traffic with ease and Eve soon had a little makeup on to at least help her feel less than a ghost of herself. By the time she tucked away her cosmetics bag, he was handing her the coffee. She cupped it between her hands as though it was the most cherished treasure, absorbing the strong aroma as she did the heat. It and the SUV's seat warmer and heater soon had her closing her eyes with pleasure. She could easily doze off again.

"That's a new technique," Derek drawled. "But I think you actually have to put the cup to your lips to get any substantive effects from the caffeine."

Snapping to attention, Eve caught his smile. "I will as soon as you park. I'm not awake enough to avoid second-degree burns."

"Ah, but I'm not parking. As it is, we're almost late."

That cleared Eve's head faster than sticking her head out the window. "Late for what?" she asked suspiciously.

"Another S.A.C. from Florida—he's an old friend from our early days at Quantico—is using his parents' cabin about forty miles from here. He and his wife asked me to come up for some snowmobiling and catching up."

From the looks of the darker clouds coming over the mountains in the west, Eve thought the weather might already be deteriorating up there. That, and the idea of dealing with Derek all day, plus another government agent was nothing close to the rest and rejuvenation that she had planned for today. "Then let me out. I'll call for a cab. No, I'll call Rae. She'll unlock the office for me and I can catch up on other projects. There's a couch there, so if we can't get back into the apartment this evening—"

"No way." Derek's tone was mild, but resolute. "I know how long it took to rouse you from sleep. What do you want to do, get seriously ill?"

"Of course not. But I don't want to intrude on your reunion, either."

"You won't. In fact, Sophie will be thrilled

to have someone to chat with while Brad and I talk shop."

Great, Eve thought. She's really going to have a lot in common with the other "god's" goddess. Wouldn't Rae have a field day with this scenario?

"I'm not dressed for this," she pleaded. She didn't want to explain just *how* underdressed she was.

"I was only kidding about the punkish hair. You look more than huggable—a little fragile from the lack of sleep, but great."

And how was he going to introduce her? She saw nothing but pitfalls before them as speculation mounted. "Don't tell them that we were neighbors back in Texas. They'll put one and one together and suggest you need therapy."

"Therapy?"

"No one is going to believe that we weren't doing the same thing that Wes and Sam were—or worse yet, playing some revenge game."

"Okay, so it would be better to tell them that I found you stranded along the road on my way up there, and plan to drop you off as soon as you figure out where it is you want to go?"

"A hitchhiking hooker?" Eve choked, torn between laughter and indignation, although she figured she would look the part if she removed her jacket, which she was committed not to do no matter how warm she got. "Nice choices. While we're cheering each other up? I'm not going on any snowmobile."

"Chicken. I drove you down the mountain half covered with ice. You know I'm careful."

"Whenever I read about an avalanche, it seems a snowmobile is involved."

"We're not about to take risks like that," Derek assured her. "Good grief, Brad and Sophie have kids to go home to."

Knowing that no matter what she said, Derek

was going to continue in the direction of the mountains, Eve turned her focus on her coffee. She would need her wits about her if she didn't want to make an utter fool of herself.

The so-called cabin was between Denver and Colorado Springs and at a higher elevation than the Graingers' house. It was almost twice the size, too. Nestled amid stately evergreens, the two-story dwelling with its floor-to-ceiling windows had a panoramic view of the Rockies.

A man as tall and fit as Derek, wearing a heavy blue-gray sweater over a gray turtleneck and jeans came out as they parked. Tanned and with blond highlights in his brown hair that spoke to his distance from his usual home, he eagerly shook hands and hauled Derek closer for a hug and back slap.

"You son of a gun. I expected you to turn us down at the last minute."

"Yeah, well, we actually had a gas leak at

the apartment complex, so it was either spend the day at a mall or come here," Derek said, as though resigned to this fate.

"Listen to you." After Brad teasingly punched him in the shoulder, he hesitated. "Wait a minute, 'we'?" He ducked for a better inspection of the confines of the SUV. "Well, hello."

With an apologetic smile, Eve wiggled her fingers back at him.

Derek leaned over to do the introductions. "Eve Easton, this is Brad Neville."

"Come on out of there," Brad told her. "This so-and-so didn't tell you we bite, did he?"

Eve took a deep breath and did as invited. She felt a little more human and less scruffy, thanks to the coffee and makeup. But like Derek, Brad looked set for a magazine shoot, and his boots were so similar to Derek's that she wondered if agents all shopped at the same stores. No doubt Sophie was equally put together and would make her want to lock herself in the nearest bathroom for the duration of this torture.

"Your place is beautiful," she said, shaking his hand. "I'm sorry for crashing your reunion, but Derek's right about what happened at our complex." She hugged her jacket closed. In her haste to comply with directives, she'd forgotten to zipper it. "As I told Derek, I'm not dressed for visiting. I had a late night." Belatedly realizing what that sounded like, she quickly added, "I mean I was working, not partying." Hearing Derek laugh softly behind her, she closed her eyes knowing that was not making things any better.

"Eve's an events planner," Derek said on her behalf. "There was a big fundraiser for a historic building last night, and she's about four hours short on sleep. Although this is generally as natural and charming as she is."

Brad's smile deepened the crow's-feet around

his hazel eyes. "I can see that. Sorry about the lost sleep, but youth clearly has its benefits. If I'd lost that much sleep, it would take a cattle prod and coffee thick enough to need a cement mixer to stir to get me on my feet. Come meet my better half."

"He means that literally," Derek added, placing his hand at the small of Eve's back to urge her forward.

Sophie Neville was her height and size, but closer to the men's ages—about five to eight years above her own thirty. She had the lovely coloring that came with Italian heritage—and a witty and warm sense of humor. After encouraging Eve twice to take off her coat, Sophie abruptly apologized for being remiss and offered to show her to a bathroom before they headed off on the snowmobiles.

Once out of earshot of the men, she took Eve's hand and led her upstairs to the master suite where she shut the door. "I'm going to talk girl to girl," she said, her brown eyes luminous with concern. "You're not comfortable at all with being here. What can I do? Are you not feeling well?"

"This is so embarrassing," Eve replied. "I was literally ordered out of bed this morning due to the leak, and they gave me no time to get properly dressed, let alone cleaned up. I thought it was okay because we'd be back shortly. Then Derek told me the bad news about how long the repairs might take. The next thing I knew we were heading up here." She parted her jacket where it was obvious she was wearing nothing beneath her sweater.

"I thought so!" Sophie pressed her hands to her chest in relief. "Poor dear. But fortunately we're not so different in size, so I can help."

She immediately went to the cherrywood dresser where she opened the drawer and in no time brought out a pretty set of silk ivory undergarments that still had the price tags on

them. "As you can see, I'd caught a sale before heading up here, so I'm happy to share."

"Oh, that's too generous," Eve protested.
"I'll write you a check right away."

"You will not. Consider it my gift in appreciation for you helping to bring Derek here. I
never liked Samantha, and Brad didn't get to
see much of Derek while they were married."

"But we're not—"

"No explanations necessary. Let's just enjoy
ourselves. I've already said more than Brad
would like me to say." As the petite, but definitely more curvaceous woman set the fine lin-
gerie on the top of the bureau, she looked from
her chest to Eve's. "You're ending up with a
little more padding than you needed, but what
can I say? Genetics." Laughing softly, she also
pulled out a pair of thick socks. "I'm sorry I
can't help you with boots, but these socks are
warmer than what I see you're wearing, and
I have plenty of extras for you to change into

when we return." Heading for the door, she said, "You make yourself at home and I'll see you downstairs when you're ready."

"I can't tell you how much I appreciate this," Eve said, genuinely touched.

"You're so very welcome."

About a half hour later, once Derek familiarized himself with the snowmobile he and Eve would be riding, he resettled astride the sleek white and blue machine, then patted the leather extended benchlike seat behind him. Eve hesitated another few seconds, but casting a resigned look at Sophie, who was already sitting behind her husband and hugging him tightly, she eased onto the machine.

Derek had driven one of these pricey motorized sleds before and was enjoying the opportunity to experience the ride again. But he couldn't deny that a good portion of his pleasure came from having Eve there with him.

"Don't be shy," he directed over his shoulder as they started off after the other red and white machine. "Put your arms around me." He'd noticed that she was looking for a good handhold on the seat, anywhere but where was most practical and safe. "I'm going to be as careful as I can, but we'll inevitably hit bumps and slip into pockets, not to mention take some sharper turns."

"Feel free not to share those kinds of details," she called above the rumble of the engine.

At first, her hold was tentative, but by the time they were a quarter mile down the trail, her arms were as tight as a vise around his middle, and she was burying her face in his back.

"You can't be that scared?" he asked with a laugh of disbelief.

"The wind stings!"

That it did, and she had far softer skin than

he did. He was grateful that Sophie had lent her a pair of orange gloves to help protect her hands, even though they clashed with her pretty red parka. They were a good idea in case they somehow got separated, too; but fat chance that he would let that happen.

"Scoot closer," he coaxed. "I have plenty of body heat."

He had to admit feeling some guilt for basically kidnapping her, but she was taking it well enough. At least she seemed to like Sophie.

"You're missing the gorgeous scenery even if it is a cloudy day."

"Are there steep drop-offs?"

"Not here."

Eve lifted her head and gasped in wonder. "Oh…it's like a Christmas card."

"We'll get a photo on your cell phone or mine to send to your family. They'd probably enjoy seeing you having a good time."

"When we stop. Will you take it with me

holding the handlebars like I'm steering? My mother was concerned that all I was doing was working through the holidays and that might reassure her."

"You bet," Derek replied, pleased to hear her starting to sound more upbeat about things.

That photo opportunity came several minutes later when they caught up with Brad and Sophie's machine where they were parked near a cut-off. Brad took a photo of both of them with Derek's BlackBerry. Then as Derek took one of her alone as she'd requested, Brad took his wife's hand.

"Soph and I are going to walk down this way a bit and see how good the trail is," Brad said. "Holler if you need rescuing, Eve."

"Some friend," Derek called after him. But as the other couple trudged off in the calf-high snow, he turned to see Eve brushing the snow from her pants and sneakers. "Damn, tuck your feet up on the seat to get them out of the snow. Are you wet through and through yet?"

"No, and it almost feels warm now that we're not moving."

He slipped his aviator-style glasses onto his head and tugged off one of his gloves to brush a little snow off the fur trimming her hood. "You're being a great sport, and you look like a cover girl."

"Are you sure your vision is good enough to drive, G-man?" Shaking her head, Eve dug out her BlackBerry from her pocket and pointed behind him. "Will you look at those clouds coming over those peaks? They almost look close enough to touch."

"That front is coming in sooner than was predicted."

"It's ethereal. I want a picture of that for my computer's desktop background."

Derek began to tease her. "I thought you didn't like the cold." But as she leaped off the machine and ran to get a better view, he grew concerned. "Evie, wait a minute. Let me do it. You're going to get soaked to the skin—and watch that drop! Eve!"

His heart lurched up into his throat as she uttered a breathless scream and dropped out of sight. Derek bolted after her braking as he spotted her some twenty feet below, her hard landing eased somewhat by the snowdrift built up against a thin cluster of sapling evergreens. But she was facedown and when she didn't move right away, he wondered if he'd been wrong about the soft landing.

"Damn—Eve!" He half loped, half skidded down the incline. Reaching her, he dropped to his knees and ran his hands over her back, her legs. "Honey? Are you all right?"

When she remained motionless, he wondered if during the fall, she'd struck her head on a snow-covered boulder or downed tree? Whether it was safe or not, he had to roll her over so she could breathe. He did so as gently as possible…and earned a face full of snow.

"Ha! Scared you, didn't I?" Her grin was irreverent. "Whew…I gave myself a pause or two. It's amazing how fast thirty years can flash before your eyes."

Derek didn't trust himself to reply. He simply wiped the snow from his face and watched her enjoy herself.

"Smile," she said, aiming her phone at him. "Uh-oh. The narrow-eyed, we-are-not-amused look."

"That's right. But this will make up for it."

Even as she realized what he intended and tried to scramble out of reach, he grabbed her by her jacket and pulled her back into his arms. She yelped and landed hard enough against his chest that, winded, she dropped onto his lap.

"Who's laughing now?" he challenged, a moment before capturing her lips with his.

The kiss immediately released an ache in

his belly and told him that he'd been living for this moment. How strange that you could see someone almost daily for years, and then one day everything changes because of a look, a turn of phrase, or a touch. Eve…she was slowly but thoroughly consuming his mind the way the clouds she'd admired were over-taking the mountains.

She was such a small woman—a little sip of water. He'd heard a native Texan—an agent—describe a fellow agent of similar build like that, and it suited Eve. He wasn't the biggest guy around, but she felt like a bird in his arms. It was a relief that a hint of her feistiness was returning. He'd seen glimpses of it before their mutual divorces, but she was often a shadow of herself in Wes's presence.

Knowing that they couldn't have long be-fore Brad and Sophie returned, Derek wasted no time in parting her lips to deepen the kiss. He was too hungry for this to wait for an-

other chance, and he sure as hell wasn't waiting for an invitation. She might flirt a little,
she was too feminine not to, but she was also
still too skittish around him to let herself be
easily caught or cornered like this again.

She tasted of coffee and the mint she'd dug
from her purse and popped in her mouth as
they'd driven up to the house. And she tasted
of Eve—sweet, a little shy, but curious, and
oh, God, tempting.

Easing onto his back, he drew her over him
and kept her there by cupping her bottom over
his undeniable arousal. Her muffled gasp had
him grinning.

"Who's laughing now?"

"Derek…we have to get back. The whole
slope could give way."

"Let it." He suckled gently on her lips as he
moved her against him. "Kiss me."

She tried not to, but he could see desire turn
her clear blue eyes the color of lapis. He felt

her arms tighten around his neck and her hips snuggle closer to cup him in ageless communication.

"Hey, you two. If you get any more neighborly, you'll melt the slope and cause an avalanche."

Derek swore in his mind, while Eve buried her face against his shoulder. Pressing a reassuring kiss against her temple, he waged the mind-over-matter battle with his body and reluctantly got them both to their feet.

"Are you all right, Eve?" Sophie called down to them. "We heard you scream. Thank goodness those young trees were there."

"I'm fine," she called back. "Sorry to give you a fright."

The steepness and slippery conditions forced her to make the climb up the slope on all fours. Derek stayed behind her as a stop-gap every time she lost ground. Then Brad positioned himself on top to grab her hand and assist her up the rest of the way.

"Got you!" he said at last, and hoisted her to level ground.

Sophie took over from there. "Your poor feet. Brad, we should head back."

"Oh, it's okay," Eve insisted. "You've hardly had a chance to see anything."

"Sit on the snowmobile," Derek told her, "and I'll get the snow that packed under your jeans." When she did as he directed, he made short work of removing the worst of the stuff, but when he tried to get off her sneakers to get the rest, she shied away.

"Really, I'm good to go," she insisted. "And we're wasting time." Her reassuring smile was for Sophie.

"There is a spectacular view down that trail," Brad said, indicating where they'd come from. "We saw one macho man of an elk."

Eve gasped. "Well, what are we doing talking about it? I've never seen one except in a zoo."

Derek didn't like this one bit. "Eve noticed the clouds." He pointed to the peaks, no longer visible. "It would probably be a good idea to get down from here while visibility is still optimum."

"Just a mile farther. There's also a place to turn that's easier than here."

Derek caught Brad's wicked grin. He was enjoying this way too much, and Eve was in fast retreat. All they needed was an earthquake to finish ruining the sweet interlude he and Eve had shared.

The elk was gone, but they did see a fox. Eve was ecstatic—until the wind picked up and snow flurries began to fall. This time Derek had no problem convincing the Nevilles to head for the house, and he never once teased Eve for keeping her face buried against his back.

By the time they pulled the snowmobiles

into the barn, Eve was frozen stiff with cold and stumbled when she tried to lift her leg over the seat. Having anticipated that she might have trouble, Derek managed to catch her, and swept her into his arms before she could seriously injure herself.

"Derek this is silly," Eve assured him. "I was just a bit stiff."

"And you'd hurt yourself proving it," he replied.

"One of *those*," Brad noted, with a sagely nod. "You have your work cut out for you, my friend."

"Mind your own business, darling," Sophie told him sweetly. To Eve she said, "It'll probably be safer if you let him get you inside. I once sprained my knee from being outdoors in the cold too long and it was months before I could get back to jogging."

She led the way inside. "Derek, if you'll get

her comfortable near the fire, I'll get dry socks and a throw to help her warm up. Brad—?"

"Feed the fire and open the wine," he replied good-naturedly. "I'm on it, babe." He winked at Eve before saying to Derek, "It's amazing that we've managed to achieve what we have in the Bureau without domestic guidance."

"I'm still within earshot," Sophie sang from the stairs.

"And I love you," he sang back.

His comical expression of panic as he raced for the wine cooler had Eve chuckling. Derek set her on one of the two ivory leather couches that faced each other, confused at the rush of jealousy he felt. The emotion was entirely foreign to him.

As he slipped off his gloves, he sat on the edge of the large carved-oak coffee table. But when he tried to remove her sneakers, Eve pulled back and lightly swatted at his hands with Sophie's borrowed gloves.

"I'm cold, not incapacitated."

"Where's your sense of romance?"

"Taking a backseat to my ticklishness." Managing to free herself, Eve bounded off the couch and hobbled and winced to the fireplace where she removed her sneakers and socks herself, then laid them on the warm stones to dry.

"You'll give yourself a concussion yet, stubborn woman," Derek muttered. Unable to give her the space she was undoubtedly trying to maintain between them, he risked another advance. "Give me your jacket and I'll hang it by the door."

At least she allowed that. With jacket in hand, he leaned down to ask in her ear, "Will you at least admit that you had a little fun?"

"Yes, of course."

"A crumb of kindness." Before she could retreat again, he kissed the side of her neck. "My life's complete."

As he carried off her parka, Brad returned with their glasses of wine. "And to think you were the best interrogator in our class at Quantico." Ignoring Derek's indecipherable response, he handed Eve her drink, adding, "Pinot noir. My money's on you, pretty lady. Drive him to distraction. Melt his memory board!"

"Brad's a Gemini," Sophie said, as she swept back into the room. "He can't resist adding his opinion, ready or not." Blowing him an air kiss, she handed Eve the pair of dry socks.

"Thanks so much," Eve said, as the brunette then wrapped a camel-colored, cashmere throw around her shoulders.

"Stay here on these warm stones," Sophie said, with an affectionate hug. "I'll get things started in the kitchen."

"Oh, I'll come help." Eve started after her.

"You will obey."

As Sophie added a pointed look to her directive, Eve, Derek and Brad froze. Brad was the first to relax.

He whispered to Eve, "This is the price you pay when your wedding guest list included distant cousins of Caesar and Tony Soprano."

"Come and help me, love of my life."

Having just finished putting new logs on the fire, he adjusted his back and thrust out his chest. "Yes, vessel of my seed, mother of my offspring." As Eve pressed fingertips to her lips, he confided, "Our second son just graduated from diapers. I can tell she's ready to try for a girl."

Eve chuckled. Once he hurried off to join Sophie, she said to Derek, "You have wonderful friends—if a little obvious."

"What's wrong with real friends hoping for the best for you?"

"Nothing. It's sweet. But you shouldn't be giving them the wrong impression about us."

Derek retrieved his glass and settled down

beside her to watch her finish slipping on her socks. "What would that be, exactly? Everything that has happened between us so far has been genuine and honest."

"I shouldn't have let you kiss me."

The words were barely audible, but they still sent a chill through Derek. "You didn't exactly have a choice—not at first. Then you liked it, too much. As much as I did." Derek knew he was going to make her uncomfortable, even embarrassed, but something was driving him and he didn't care. It was a risk he felt worth taking. "No, that's impossible. Not possibly as much as me."

Eve picked up her glass and stared into the nearly opaque burgundy liquid as though it was a crystal ball. "Derek—"

"I want you, Eve. I want to make love with you."

"Warning," Brad announced, returning with

a tray. "Envious guy nearly in the dog house approaching."

Eve all but launched from her perch. "I'm going to go help Sophie."

Derek knew there was no stopping her, unless he wanted Eve to make good her escape this time, and Brad settled where she'd been sitting and offered the platter of canapés to Derek. "Why haven't I heard of her before?"

"Because this is new...although she was married to the man my ex is now married to."

"Holy—pardon." Brad took a generous sip of his wine. "Uh, so you've known each other awhile?"

"Get that idea out of your head. Yes, we were neighbors, and as she'll tell you herself, we didn't do more than say hi and exchange reactions to the weather in all of that time."

Brad studied Eve in the kitchen. "She's a doll. You expect me to believe that?"

"I didn't walk away from a window if she

happened to be outside," Derek said, remembering. "But did I instigate what my ex did with her ex? No."

"So she didn't know you got this position up here?" Brad asked.

Derek thought back to that special night. "We ended up at the same New Year's Eve party and she did everything but run screaming into the night. I'm trying to get her to give me the benefit of the doubt."

Brad sipped again. "She's an innocent—in a good way. That has to be refreshing. You've been fighting the mistake that was Sam for a long time."

"So much for my poker face."

"Yeah, well, I introduced you two," Brad reminded him. "Guilt is my middle name." He bowed his head for several seconds, then asked, "What did you say she does? Events planner? I would have guessed preschool teacher."

"You're not far off."

"Have you introduced her to your handcuffs yet?"

Derek elbowed him in the ribs.

"I didn't like Brad when I met him," Sophie announced out of the blue.

Although Eve studiously continued to toss the salad she'd prepared, she indulged in a wary glance toward the living room. She could see that Derek and Brad were deep in conversation, which was a relief considering Sophie's pronouncement.

"Well, you fooled me. You're so clearly in love," Eve said softy.

"Now. Earlier on it was simple attraction. Lust. I listened to my Aunt Sophie, whom I was named after," Sophie explained. "She was the scandalous one in the family. She had countless lovers before she settled down with my uncle, who was a playboy and made it clear that he couldn't limit himself to just one woman. Brad was a bit of a playboy himself," she said, pausing as she stood before the tuna she was searing. "Do you know what she said to him? 'I don't compete, and I don't share.' He never saw another woman again. That's what changed my life with Brad. Aunt Sophie's wisdom," she said, with a serene smile.

Eve came to watch Sophie plate her homemade pasta. "But you're beautiful and vibrant. I can't imagine that you ever had to worry."

"I know that now. I didn't as a younger woman. Society plays with our hearts and instincts." She slid Eve a knowing look. "You don't have to worry about Derek, either."

"But we aren't—"

"No, not yet. I can see as much. But he wants you. That's a compliment. Derek has always been a one-woman man, even when he no longer loved that woman. His word is everything to him. Most women don't know what a gift that is. I think you do, Eve."

Although it was late and the snow was blowing nearly horizontally as they headed home, Eve was too soothed by the wine she'd drunk to be very anxious. She'd enjoyed herself more than she had since moving up here. Except maybe for New Year's Eve.

"You're lucky to have such good friends that you can be apart from for so long and within minutes slip right back into that groove," she said, as she took one last glance back at the house.

"It was that way from the moment we met," he replied, never taking his eyes off of the road. "You seemed to really take to Sophie."

"What's not to enjoy? She's tiramisu after a wedding banquet. I've never met anyone like her."

"Her entire family is the same way. They

own one of the most prestigious vineyards in California."

Eve gasped. "Good grief! She said nothing about that."

Derek smiled.

"I must have come off as a small-town hick to her."

"She whispered to me that she now might forgive me for having ever married Sam."

Eve knew he'd shared that to make her feel more secure about having been included in their day, but the assumption that they were now in a relationship had the opposite effect. "I'd like to send her a note if you would give me their address?"

"I will. What's wrong?"

"Nothing. I guess I'm finally feeling the lost sleep." She pretended to stifle a yawn. "That was good wine, too. I take it that it's from the family vineyard?"

"It was."

"There's something else I'd like to add to my note. I wish I'd paid more attention to the label."

"Knowing Sophie, she'll make a point to send you a bottle or two once she knows where to send it."

"How did she and Brad meet?"

"He was a motorcycle cop and was involved in a hit-and-run accident. She witnessed it and managed to get enough of the perpetrator's license to get the guy arrested. The rest was history—at least for Brad it was. But when he asked her out, she turned him down. She was in a relationship. Funny thing is that their paths kept crossing and, when she came upon him after he'd had another accident, she stopped and said she'd go out with him if he gave up the bike. She was convinced he was going to end up killing himself. He said he would do it if she would marry him."

"She must be much happier with him being

with the Bureau than riding city streets and the interstate on a high-powered bike," Eve said, certain that she would have felt the same way. "Especially now that he's in the position that he's in. I mean—I guess I shouldn't ask this, but you're not out and about risking life and limb as you did when you were a field agent, are you?"

"No."

Eve cast him a covert look sensing he wasn't saying everything he was thinking. "With Brad being over at the Miami office, and Sophie's family in California, it must be hard on her to be so far from family."

"She loves Brad. They've created their own family now."

Remembering that Sophie said their two sons were staying with grandparents, Eve thought about how difficult the holidays had to be trying to get the entire family together. "Brad's parents must live in Florida, since school has started again?"

"They do. Brad's father owned one of the biggest boat dealerships in Florida before he retired. His mother hosted a local TV show until she started her own home decorating line."

"Good grief—that's why I recognized some things in the master suite. Liz Neville of Neville's Nesting is Brad's mother! I just gave Sela something from her collection for her birthday."

"Brad and Sophie will be pleased that you're not only familiar with her product, but like her style, as well."

Derek reached across the console to squeeze the hand she rested on her thigh. Eve was acutely aware how that minimal touch sent her body into sensory overload. Her pulse raced, she grew flushed, and her heart fluttered like a baby bird's wings. But her mind reacted in the exact opposite way, sending up roadblocks and being cynical.

Be sensible. You're not as brave or generous as Sophie. You're not what Derek needs or deserves.

When they pulled into the complex, it was a relief to see that the yellow police tape was gone. Derek had called earlier, so they knew that it would be safe to return to their homes; however, actually seeing everything looking unchanged after the morning's commotion made what had happened earlier seem like a dream. Although it was only a little after nine o'clock, there were few lights on in apartments, and yet the parking lot was almost full. Either people were watching TV in the dark, or the day's excitement had exhausted them, and they'd turned in early.

"Rather anticlimactic, isn't it?" Derek asked, as though reading her mind.

"That's fine with me." They had exited his

SUV and were starting up the walkway, now covered with a dusting of fresh snow. Eve felt increasingly jittery. She just knew what was coming.

As they approached her door, Derek slipped his fingers through hers. Once they stopped, he studied them, while stroking her with his thumb. His touch on her bare ring finger caused a jolt that she couldn't repress.

Although his gaze lifted to hers, proving he'd noticed, he didn't release her; rather, he drew her into his arms. When he kissed her, it was slow and deep with none of the rushed urgency of this morning.

Eve couldn't resist this one last time. She wanted him. His touch made her feel more alive than anyone had before. The wind had a bite and the snow blowing under the porch stung, but she felt warm and safe in his strong arms. It had been a long, cold year, until Derek, yet she'd had no problem resisting the offers she'd received from men. She hadn't been interested in a fling. Derek wanted more—he'd said as much the night they'd had dinner, and she could see it in his eyes as he lifted his head to speak.

Her heart heavy, she made herself back away. "I can't," she whispered.

Derek sighed, but tenderly brushed snow from her cheek. "It's too soon. I understand."

"I'm not a tease, or a prude." Eve clenched her hands to keep from reaching out to lay her palm against his chest in an appeal to make him understand. But touching would send the wrong message. All she could do was try to find the words to make him accept what she felt. "It's just that I don't think we should be starting something that will only cause hurt down the road."

"Give us a chance," he said quietly. "I'd never throw Wes in your face, and I know you'd never use Sam against me. No, wait," he continued, when she began to protest. "I know next you're going to warn that you might return to Texas. That's starting to be your M.O. as soon as you realize you're actually enjoying being with me or feeling something. But what if we're so good together that leaving ceases to be an option?"

She knew what she should say to end this quickly, but she couldn't make herself do it. She wasn't going to be cruel to be kind. "What if you get transferred or promoted or whatever is next for someone in your field?" she asked instead. Then she watched him as he contemplated the question that he had less or no control over.

"We'd talk it over," he began. "But I won't lie to you, that's what happens with the Bureau. With most government positions. We relocate. We adjust. Because we believe in what we do."

Feeling as though her heart was draining of blood, Eve gentled her tone. "I don't want that kind of life. I'm already too far away from my family. As an only child, I don't expect you to understand, but it's different for me. I tried to prove to myself that I could take it in stride and be pragmatic about it, but I'm just kidding myself."

Derek looked crestfallen. "I see."

"I'm sorry," she whispered.

"So am I." Derek shoved his hands into his pockets. "I guess there's nothing else to say except, go on and do what you have to do. Run home, little girl."

Chapter Five

Over the next several days, Eve wouldn't have minded catching the flu—virtually anything else in order to avoid Rae's inevitable third degree about Derek. However, she managed to avoid any and every illness. It was as if *she* was the toxic one. It was just as well, she eventually concluded. Angie had started maternity leave and she couldn't in good conscience leave everyone in a bind.

The inevitable questioning happened the following Wednesday shortly after they'd received the call from Angie saying she'd given birth to a healthy boy that they'd named Adam. Eve had come into Rae's office and they sat updating their monthly planners with the latest contracted events. Despite being increasingly busy, this weekend they actually had a four-day lull.

"If Gus can break away, I think we'll head up to the mountains and hibernate," Rae said. "On the other hand, I haven't had this kind of opportunity to play in my workshop since before Thanksgiving." She glanced across her desk at Eve. "Why don't you take off, too? The others can manage the office. I'll bet if you let Mr. Special Agent-in-Charge know that you had the time off, he might see this as a perfect opportunity to sweep you away on a romantic interlude."

Leave it to Rae to take one dinner and turn things into a flaming affair. Eve wished she had never confided about the night at the bistro to her. If she'd mentioned Saturday in the mountains with Derek's friends, Rae would have them all but engaged.

"If you're giving me the time off, I'll catch a flight to Texas and see the family," she told her, as she studiously finished penning data into her planner.

"Invite Derek to go with you."

The tip of Eve's pen almost slid off the page. She looked up to see Rae watching her way too suspiciously. "Okay...you know I'm not going to do that, but...how do you know that's not going to happen?"

"I ran into him on Monday. I was heading for the luncheon appointment with my banker, and he was leaving the same place." Rae shook her head slowly. "He looked so sad."

"No, he didn't." Eve wasn't going to be tricked into saying too much.

"I know when a man is licking wounds committed by another woman."

Not even wanting to have this conversation, Eve scrunched her eyes closed. "Please tell me that you didn't pry him with questions?"

"I did not. I just said that you'd been very quiet all morning, which you were. Then he said he was feeling that way himself and that you'd basically told him to go away."

"I couldn't think of what else to do. Things were getting serious. I don't want to hurt him. I care for him—very much."

Rae set her chin on her folded hands looking sympathetic, but perplexed. "Then what's the problem?"

Derek didn't tell her? Of course he hadn't. Unlike Wes, he was a man of honor. He wouldn't betray the admission she'd shared in confidence. He would leave her to tell Rae her decision about her future when she'd made it. That had Eve experiencing another pang of regret and she had to bow her head as she struggled not to tear up. "I don't expect you to understand."

"But I'd like to try. Are you afraid?" Rae shrugged, her expression philosophical. "You have a right to be. That doesn't mean you stop living."

"But he's government, Rae. What if he gets transferred one day? I don't want to live in Washington, D.C., or even farther from home."

"Home is where your heart beats with the sweetest rhythm, darling." Rae fingered the double strand of pearls resting in the neck-line of her navy blue suit and studied Eve as though she was a new life species. "If Gus told me tomorrow that he wanted to start building beach houses on the Carolina coast, I'd put this business and our houses on the market— after I had him checked out by a doctor. He's my world, and I'm only half a person without him."

Eve was grateful that she'd shut the door to

Rae's office because she didn't want the others to hear any of this. "But that's what I took into consideration before Derek and I discovered that we were heading to such deep feelings. I want to give him a chance to find someone who is better suited to the life he's chosen."

"There's just one detail you're overlooking— he clearly wants *you*." Rae's expression grew troubled. "What happens if this was it for you? What if having been treated so shabbily by Wes, that you were being given this gift—a man who is going to adore you as you deserve to be adored? Only this is it, this is your window of opportunity and there aren't going to be any other chances because he was the *one*. Are you going to be okay at forty or sixty or eighty being alone? You know the rest of your family is going to move on. I'm sure they're missing you, too, but the sad truth is that all of us are expendable. That's what life and death are all about. Before we can get too big for our britches, life or destiny, or whatever you want to call it, comes along and gives you a punch somewhere when you least expect it, so you can get your priorities straight."

Eve closed her planner and hugged it to her chest. "That's all very sensible, but—" she gave Rae a sudden, worried look "—you aren't about to tell me that you're ill, are you?"

"No, sweetie. But I was. I'm a three-year cancer survivor and it changed my life. I can still be afraid of what tomorrow holds, but I don't starve myself of love and life to play it safe. I understand that not everyone was born to be a globe-trotter," she continued, "but hear me on this. As long as you're with the person who means everything to you, how awful could a relocation be?"

"I can't have this discussion." Eve rose and headed for the door. "You're very dear to me, but I just can't."

"If he's half the man I think he is, Derek won't give up," Rae warned.

Eve shook her head. She knew Rae was wrong on that one. "He was so disappointed in me. He's concluded that I'm too immature for him. He as much as said it."

Rae replied with a feminine snort. "Eve, you dialogue with mayoral staff and top executives every day. Why would you let him get away with saying something like that?"

"Because he's not wrong." At Rae's incredulous look, she continued, "I can represent you, fight for you, work for *you* easily. You're the whole package. I believe in you. At best, I'm Rae light. I don't have that foundation of—of—"

"Confidence?"

"For myself? No," Eve admitted. "I was going to say education and social connections, but in the end it is confidence, isn't it?" She hated that Rae was clearly not happy with what she was hearing; however, having gotten this far, she would finish. "I bought into Wes and invested greatly, you know that from our early days together and our chats. But I was never good enough. Although from what Derek has confided about Samantha, I don't see how Wes thinks he got a better deal."

"Never mind him," Rae muttered. "You're who I care about. You've become like a kid sister to me. I'd say daughter, but I'm too vain."

Eve couldn't help but smile. "I'm seriously fond of you, too."

"Does your family know anything about this? Anything about Derek and denying your future happiness for their sake?"

"Good grief, no!"

Eve could imagine her father's reaction to the idea that she had gone out with Sam's ex: *"What's wrong with him? She didn't want him. She wanted your husband, and we all know what a prize he turned out to be."*

"Well, I think you should go home," Rae told her. "I think you should tell them how you feel and what you did, and then see what happens."

Eve knew what Rae thought she was setting her up for, but she was giddy as a kid on her birthday as she landed at Houston Intercontinental Airport, picked up her rental car and headed north toward her parents' home. The temperature was a balmy 62°F, the skies were cerulean blue, and she could barely resist picking up her BlackBerry to call them and announce, "Guess where I am?"

The miles flew by despite the heavy traffic. She was in her element, in her home territory. She couldn't wait to spend the rest of the day catching up and hugging everyone. She planned to make them the nectarine crisp that Honor had introduced her to during their week-long Christmas celebration at the office. First thing in the morning, she would have breakfast with all four of her grandparents. Later she would drive her father around on the golf cart and watch him play a few holes, then kidnap her mother for a manicure pampering.

She had arrived at the family home just after ten o'clock and was shocked to see her parents loading her grandparents into their van. Loading, as in—luggage included.

"Evie!" Having reached her first, her mother had her in a bear hug before she had both legs out of the rental. "What are you doing here? What a wonderful surprise!"

Eve beamed at the woman who was her height and coloring, and looked at least a decade younger than her years, especially in her pink jogging suit. "That was the idea. Where are you going?"

"Branson."

"Missouri?" Eve all but squeaked.

"That's the one with all the action. We have tickets for two shows already. Your father won fourth place in the seniors tournament. We're so excited."

"But I just flew down. I have all weekend." She went over to the van to hug her father. "Hi, Daddy." Then she crawled around the van on her knees to kiss her grandparents. "Hi-Hi-Hi-Hi!"

"You should have called, sweetheart," her father said, returning to the task of putting luggage in the back. His dark brown hair barely had any gray showing in it, and his year-round tan hadn't faded a bit despite the season. "But you brought your key, right? Make yourself at home and catch up with friends. You probably need the sleep anyway."

"I don't. I wanted to catch up with you."

"Come with us then," Grandpa Easton said.

"There's room," Grandpa Leeland chimed in.

"When are you coming back?" Eve asked, although she didn't want to spend that many hours in a vehicle, or go to see shows she had no interest in.

"Next Wednesday," Grandma Leeland announced. "I have a dental checkup."

"I have to be back at work on Monday," Eve said, with an apologetic smile.

Her father came to her again and gave her another hug and kiss. "Go see your sister. She was whining yesterday about being too fat to fit in any of her clothes and needing a crane to get up from a chair."

Nice, Eve thought, feeling increasingly deflated. She was reduced to being a slot filler. "Okay, I guess I'll do that. Have a safe trip and a great time."

She watched as they finished loading, then waved them off.

As soon as they were out of sight, her brave smile vanished. She couldn't believe it. The tickets had to be good for more than one date. Why didn't they reschedule?

Feeling more than a little dejected, she called her sister. "Hey," she said more cheerfully than she felt. "Want some company?"

"My water is about to break at any minute, Eve. I look like a beached whale, and my assistant just screwed up a major piece of documentation. I'm not sure I'd be good company. Where are you?"

"I'm at the folks', but they just left for Branson for fun and games with the grands, so I thought I'd head your way and help out if I can."

"Bless you. Did I happen to mention that my sitter is sick? Your timing is perfect."

Three hours later she pulled into her sister's driveway just as her brother-in-law was assisting Sela into her Mercedes. As Eve ran to them, Mitchell gave her a quick kiss on the cheek and handed her a set of keys to the house. "The contractions are coming fast and furious. Baby Evagail has done nothing expected. Zach is with the neighbor. She knows you were on your way. Tell your sister to breathe, please. She's tuned out my voice."

Eve ducked into the car to kiss her older sister's cheek. "Breathe. Do you want me to call the folks?"

"Mitch will do it when she's out. Great timing, kiddo, thanks!"

And that was how Eve spent her four days off. By the time she drove back to Houston on Sunday, Sela was home with her second child, daughter Evagail, named after Eve and Mitch's sister Gail, surrounded by Mitch and three-year-old Zach. They'd been the picture of happiness, and Eve had felt like the third or rather fifth wheel once more. What a learning experience!

It wasn't that she regretted the trip. In fact she had that talk Rae wanted her to have.

But she wasn't prepared for how strongly she would be affected by it.

It was before dawn on Sunday morning and she'd heard movement down the hall, so she'd gone to see if she could be of some help. She found Sela in the nursery nursing Evagail.

Sela's hair was cascading around her shoulders. She was a brunette like their father and had his hazel eyes. Since she usually wore her gorgeous, lush locks in some braid or twist, she looked much younger and approachable than the cool and contained attorney she was at the office.

"You make such a beautiful picture," Eve said, lowering herself to the carpet to watch.

"Thanks. Listen to this little piggy eat," Sela said, though her eyes were bright with love. The subtle sucking sounds were interspersed with tiny grunts. "She's going to have my addiction to anything with calories."

"Sis, you always look like a million bucks,

even when heavy with child." Eve wasn't being falsely complimentary, either. Sela's skin was luminous during her pregnancies, and there was a radiant grace about her like she knew some secret that no one else did. "And, excuse me, but I saw how Mitchell was looking at you as he helped you get to the car when you were in labor. The man is still besotted after two children and ten years of marriage. That's rare in my book."

Sela shook her head, but smiled. "I'm sorry you have to leave. I finally have the energy and time to visit."

"Yeah, right. Maybe after the kids are out of college," Eve mused.

While Sela acknowledged that possibility via a half shrug, she studied Eve in the glow of the nightlight. "I'm sorry that you didn't get some time with the folks."

"Well, things seem to have worked out the way they needed to, and I got to see my little namesake before they did, 'nah-nah-nah,'" she sang.

But Sela didn't laugh as Eve intended. "So when are you going to tell me why you really came down?"

"I was homesick. I wanted to see my family."

"Poor baby sis. Nicholas and I couldn't wait to spread our wings and launch ourselves from the nest, and your favorite place is always there. Sometimes I think you married Wes because he didn't mind if you went home for an extended weekend visit the way another possessive spouse might have resented it." As soon as the words were out, Sela saw Eve's expression change and clapped her hand over her mouth. "Oh, God. I'm sorry."

"No, you're right." Eve mocked herself by making an L with her thumb and index finger and held it to her forehead. There was no denying the truth. "Wes used my absences to start his affair with Sam. I'm so gullible, I thought when I found one of her casserole dishes in my dishwasher, she really did want to be a good neighbor and had made an extra for him while I was out of town. It also took me longer than it probably would most women to realize that the reason I was running out of laundry soap so fast wasn't because Wes poured in too much when he did his own workout clothes. He was getting the sheets clean and back on the bed, too."

"Stop," Sela entreated, looking away. "I'm having such bad thoughts about that scumbag that my milk might sour."

"You're the best sister a divorcée could have," Eve said with a grin. "But I've thought enough dark thoughts for the both of us."

Sela shook her head. "You're trying to divert me. You've been very quiet since I've gotten back. Is something wrong at work?"

"Work is pretty cool. We're busy. My boss

is still pushing me with the French as with everything else."

"Mais comment est votre énonciation?" Sela asked of her enunciation.

"Presque aussi bon que le vôtre, chère mère de ma nièce," Eve replied, hoping her sister agreed, despite not having used her high school French until she'd moved to Colorado.

Sela's surprise was praise enough. "Well done, Evie. This job is obviously a good fit for you."

"If only it wasn't so far away."

"Which brings me back to my original question—what's wrong?"

Eve decided that she might as well get her wise sister's perspective. "I broke off a relationship."

"You were in a relationship already?" Sela asked with some bemusement.

"What do you mean already? I've been divorced for a year."

"But every time we talked, you said there was no one. At Christmas you said you weren't dating anyone at all."

"I met him at the New Year's party."

"And it's already over?" Sela looked worried. "He wasn't abusive, was he?"

"No! No—no. He's lovely. But he's FBI and—"

"You broke off a relationship with an FBI agent?" As the baby protested her louder tone, Sela soothed the little bundle, until Evagail went back to nursing. "Mitchell will disown you as a sister-in-law."

Eve belatedly remembered that her ex-Army Reserve brother-in-law had wanted to apply to the FBI, but family commitments—namely Sela's great job with her company—had made him go into local law enforcement instead to ensure there would be no relocation problems.

"He's actually Special Agent-in-Charge of

the Denver office," she said, as though tip-toeing on eggshells.

Sela stopped rocking. "You're determined to leave me speechless, aren't you? What a quirk of fate that slut-zilla's ex was FBI, too. I wonder if they know each other? Well, Sam's ex would know *of* him. My company does a good deal of computer intel work and I know our area's Special Agent-in-Charge." Sela began rocking again. "I can see you charming the pants off a guy like that."

"Sela!"

"That was a compliment, sis. You always underestimated your strengths. Visually, you're a delight and yet unthreatening to women. Believe me, as a woman other women love to hate, I get this. But then you have a sweet, but genuine and quirky perseverance. You're a natural organizer and leader. *You* made Wes look better than he was. To a guy like your

Special Agent-in-Charge, you would be the ultimate wet dream."

"I am going to cover Evagail's ears if you don't," Eve said, rising to her knees.

"Okay, okay, sit. Talk. Now I'm dying to know what went wrong."

Eve sat down again. She was still trying to digest the huge compliments her sister had paid her. To tell her the truth now was going to make all that a joke. She was beginning to see as much herself. "Please don't laugh too loud or fuss at me. I know we're diametrically different in big ways. But this comes from the heart."

"Of course it does, sweetie. You *are* our family's heart. I've said it to Mom and Dad repeatedly over the years."

"You did?"

Sela nodded. "Do you think the grands would all be living so close as they are if you hadn't made them believe in the idea? And

Nicholas and I would be on opposite coasts if not for you pulling on our heartstrings."

"I'm thinking of moving back to Texas," Eve said before her sister made it impossible for her to speak.

"Because...?"

"Because I'm homesick."

Sela gazed down at her new daughter and seeing that she'd gone to sleep, she returned the child to her crib, and then drew Eve over to the loveseat by the bay window. "You are our Christmas tree star," she said, wrapping her arms around her. "I should have guessed you would be miserable so far away."

"Sela, I was born in May. I'm the stubborn bull."

"Nope. You're the generous and persevering idealist. That's wonderful, but life often works against ideals and we have to make do with what is there." She kissed Eve's temple. "I would love to have you here to bond with

Evagail, and to keep Mitch from giving Zach an ulcer before he graduates from T-ball. I know you would sacrifice your weekends to chauffeur the grands from discount store to garage sale for things they don't need. I'm telling you straight out, if you do that for us, you would break my heart. More important, you would break your own heart because you won't be living the life you were meant to have."

Sela was telling her what she'd already surmised this weekend. She wasn't needed. Wanted, undoubtedly. But everyone was okay here, Eve realized. They would adapt and thrive with or without her. This discovery had been educational, but not without a lot of disappointment and some hurt.

"Okay, I guess I better tell you the rest of it," she told Sela. "My former next-door neighbor? The agent?"

"Yes."

"Derek is Special Agent-in-Charge."

"No!" Sela whispered.

"It gets better—or worse." She told her sister how they met and then the shock on the drive home as they learned they were neighbors again.

"He's right," Sela said when Eve was finished with her story. "You can't continue thinking the way you have been." But the way she studied Eve was disconcerting. "He sounds like such a dish. Are you being honest with me about there being nothing between you when you lived down here?"

"Sela, I refused to go out with him at first because I knew people would think exactly that. Nothing could be further from the truth."

"I believe you." Her sister bit her lower lip. "What are you going to do?"

"Nothing. I blew it. I cringe just remembering his expression." Eve laid her head on Sela's shoulder. "Turning thirty sucks. I'm never going to get as smart as you or stop having so many regrets."

"Being intelligent and ambitious can be as frustrating as it is fun," Sela replied, humor entering her voice. "I'll never be Minister of the Moon. I'm figuring in twenty years, we'll colonize the place and they'll need government. Why not me? Only I'm too selfish to miss watching my daughter getting her doctorate in some technology that doesn't have a name yet. Whoever said you *can* have it all was full of it."

"Poor overachiever," Eve said, laughing softly. "Why didn't we talk this way a few years ago?"

"Because you were a twit married to a bombastic egomaniac."

Choking, Eve gasped. "Tell me what you really think!"

Sela shushed her. "Here's my twenty cents worth of advice, and then I'm going to bed before the urchin over there decides she's hungry again. I think you have been heading in the right direction since you drove up to Denver. Just stop letting the past get in your way."

By the time Eve got home from work on Monday, she was tired as she'd ever been. Everything that could go wrong at the office did, and the girls had used the absence of Rae and herself to do who knew what, except catching up on work. Be that as it may, once she pulled into the complex parking lot, she was hopeful. She'd decided to talk to Derek.

It was almost dusk, and Derek's SUV wasn't there yet, but the complex manager was at the mailboxes. Hoping he would pull in while she was getting her mail, she went over to join the young blond in the plum ski jacket and matching wool slacks.

"Hi, Yvette," she said, smiling at the usually friendly thirty-something.

"Eve. Good to run into you. Your lease expires soon, too. You need to come in and renew in the next few weeks, okay?"

That's when Eve noticed the manager was using a key on Derek's box. "Um, okay. Will do. Is something wrong with Derek's box?"

"No, he just moved." The woman bundled the mail with a rubber band and slipped her keys back into her jacket pocket. "He was missing a few items and asked me to check his box since he'd already turned in the key."

"I can't believe it," Eve murmured mostly to herself. Then she realized Yvette was studying her with some curiosity. "I mean, I just talked to him last week."

"Sometimes it happens that way."

"Where has he relocated to?"

That blunt question earned her another look. "We don't share personal information unless directed to do so. I can pass on that you asked about him if you want? He should be coming by tomorrow to pick up this." She gestured with the bundle of mail.

Eve knew she was just following orders, but she also sensed a little coolness in Yvette's tone and suspected any message would be promptly forgotten. Was she interested in Derek, too? Trying to be discreet, she opened her own mailbox and in the process dropped her gaze to Yvette's hands. Her ring finger was bare.

"Oh, no." She pulled out the single piece of junk mail and locked up again. "Thanks, though. I would have just wished him the best. You have a good evening," she added, and made a hasty escape.

Gone! Eve returned to her apartment in shock. She couldn't believe that Derek wouldn't have at least said goodbye. Had he been so upset with her to make such a snap decision, and then moved out so quickly? She knew he was renting his furniture and she supposed it had been removed while she'd been at work. It would only take him an hour or two to get his personal belongings. Could this mean his feelings had gone deeper than even she had imagined?

As she closed herself in her dark apartment, she leaned against the door all but hyperventilating. She felt as though the air was being sucked out of the room.

"Now you've done it," she whispered.

"Why are you on my case?" Lisa Hart demanded of Eve, the moment they were alone at the ticket table. The sultry brunette adjusted the deep V-necked ivory sweater over her designer jeans, and challenged her with her haughty brown glare.

"You're supposed to stay here to sell tickets to dunk our celebrity athletes," Eve replied, keeping her voice as calm as possible. Even though there was a lot of music and laughter going on in the hotel and convention center, people picked up on negative vibes quickly. "But for most of the Dunk and Donate event, you've been over by the tank flirting with the guys. You don't hustle on Rae's dime. And for the record, number 36 is engaged and his fiancée is the niece of the mayor."

"You're just jealous," Lisa replied. "I didn't see anyone trying to get your phone number. Besides, Rae knows I took this job to meet people."

"Yes, but not if you cost her a future client. I'm not going to warn you again."

Offended, Lisa flipped her long hair over her shoulder, almost slapping Eve. She retreated to the opposite end of the table and immediately beamed at a young soldier. "Hey there, good-looking. I'll bet you have a strong pitching arm. It's five dollars for three throws to dunk our Broncos into that tank. And you get a free entry for a cruise."

Nodding in approval, Eve said to the people within hearing distance, "We're gearing up for the big drawing, everyone. They're one dollar, or come free if you buy a chance at the dunking pool. Who hasn't filled out their stubs?" She took a dollar from a man. "Thank you, sir. Put your name and phone number on the tickets. Someone *will* win a cruise tonight!"

The event was part of a Denver Gives Back program, and they were one of at least a dozen displays in the huge lobby. One of the largest churches was selling Valentine's gifts to raise money for the local food bank, a fire department from the suburbs of Denver was splitting profits from their calendar to an area veteran rehabilitation facility, and for a donation, the hospital was giving free screenings for several health issues. But from what Eve could tell, their booth, that they were operating for the Denver Broncos, was clearly making the most impact and money tonight.

Eve was feeling the pace and stress of the week taking its toll on her, and she was grateful when Honor offered to relieve her so she could open a bottle of water and give her throat a break. She'd been talking nonstop for the past two hours.

After taking two long drinks, she checked her watch, reassuring herself that they would start shutting down in another forty minutes. Then she saw that Lisa had slipped away again. The brash beauty was back at the dunking booth, now intruding as some players were signing autographs for young kids. With a shake of her head, she knew she would have to report this to Rae. She didn't want anyone to lose a job in today's economic environment, but she couldn't let Lisa get away with disrespecting her, either.

Then, as though that wasn't enough, in between the spectators, she spotted a couple leaving the hotel's restaurant on the far side of the lobby. Derek? And the woman looked enough like Sam to give Eve whiplash.

He wouldn't! Oh, Derek...anyone but a woman who could be Sam's clone.

She watched him help her slip into her coat, and then they looked around at the activities in the lobby. As they turned her way, Eve quickly spun away not wanting to be seen staring. She smiled shakily at an elderly man, who handed her a dollar bill and proceeded to fill out a ticket.

"Thank you, sir. I hope you win."

When she thought it was safe, she looked back and Derek and the woman were exiting the building.

For the rest of that last hour, she felt like she was trapped in a fog, her vision blurred by hurt. If Honor hadn't reminded her, she might have forgotten they had to do the drawing. She gave her the honors—something that annoyed Lisa, since she'd returned in the hopes of getting to stand before the microphone and have her five seconds of maximum attention. After that, Lisa left, failing to do her share of closing down their display and boxing things away.

By the time Eve started driving home, she was blinking away tears.

Okay, she told herself. Derek was doing exactly what she'd told him to do—moving on. But did he have to do it so fast, and with a woman like *that?*

When she finally fell asleep, she dreamed of him. It was the night they'd returned from the mountains and his parting words were more of a sneer this time.

She woke shaken and with her pillow wet from tears. "I was wrong," she moaned, curling into a tight ball of misery. "I was so wrong."

Chapter Six

"So what are you going to do about it?" Lisa announced boldly in Rae's office.

It was the last Monday in January, and Eve was several minutes late in arriving due to an accident that blocked her from leaving her apartment complex. She hadn't slept well all weekend, and she definitely wasn't ready for Lisa taking advantage and trying to justify her behavior at the event on Friday night.

"Eve is my assistant," Rae stated—and not for the first time. "You know that at these things, she has my full confidence and authority to direct any and all of you. If she felt that you weren't doing your fair share—and you forget, dear, I've spoken to you before about excessive flirting—then there must have been justification."

As Eve laid her purse and briefcase on her desk, and began unbuttoning her coat, she watched Lisa square her shoulders. *Uh-oh,* Eve thought. *Here it comes.*

"It's not fair. I've been here longer. I should have been made assistant. Besides, I sold more tickets in fifteen minutes than she and Honor did together."

"Which, of course, had nothing to do with the cut of your sweater," Eve said, entering Rae's office. "Would you like the door closed?" she asked her.

Rae glanced through the window at the others, who weren't making the slightest pretense of not eavesdropping. "No, I think we're about done here." To Lisa, she added calmly, "We'll miss you, of course, but if you're not happy here, then you need to move on to someplace that better suits your goals. What I will do is give you the day off to think about it. You're an extremely attractive young woman and when you can contain yourself, you're an asset to this company. But you're too easily swayed by your passions. That's why you weren't offered the position."

Tears of indignation flooded Lisa's eyes. "Now that you've humiliated me in front of *her,* how am I supposed to continue working here?"

"By being the mature young woman that I thought I'd hired."

"I'll take that day," Lisa snapped and walked out. She barely paused to grab her jacket and purse, and rushed from the office.

Eve waited until the front door eased shut behind her before quietly closing Rae's. "I'm sorry. I'd hoped she'd realize over the weekend that she'd made a big mistake, but apparently something else is going on with her."

"Yes, PMS," Rae muttered. She took a sip of coffee from her mug and grimaced. "Tepid already, and I loathe nuked coffee."

"Considering how supportive you were of me and my position, I'll happily go over to the café and buy you a cappuccino or espresso."

"Thanks, but I really have had enough caffeine. Sit down and tell me what has you looking like you've been hugging the porcelain throne all weekend? Did you catch a bug?"

Although Eve sat, she was less eager to respond. She wasn't sure she was ready to fill Rae in on what else had happened. They hadn't really had a chance to catch up since she'd returned from Texas, except for her to show off a photo of her new niece, Evagail. Besides, she'd spent all weekend brooding and feeling weepy. It was time for that maturity that Rae expected of them.

"Wow, it must be bad," Rae said quietly, as she watched her.

"Derek moved. I thought I saw his SUV when I returned from my trip," she said, replaying the scene in her mind. "But on Monday when I got home, he was gone."

"Moved where?"

"That's on a need-to-know basis, and our complex manager didn't think I needed to know."

After a lift of her arched eyebrows, Rae tapped her finger against her coral lips. "Moved. How titillating."

Eve didn't pretend to understand. "How so?"

"If he didn't care, why inconvenience himself to such an extent?"

No, Eve thought, she was wrong. "He cares so much, he went out on a date Friday night."

Rae lowered her gaze to her desk, a small

frown forming between her eyebrows. "I see. So he attended the event?"

"No, they dined at the lobby restaurant. Oh, Rae—" hearing the hitch in her voice, Eve swallowed "—she could have been Samantha's twin."

"You don't think it was her, do you?"

Eve shook her head. "Sam is pregnant with Wes's child. I'm guessing she would be showing by now. And besides, considering how hard she worked to get Wes, would she have left him? Also, from everything Derek said and intimated, taking her back would never be an option."

"Then why take out a woman who will inevitably remind him of her?" Rae's eyes lit with a new thought. "Could he have known you were there? Did he purposely arrange something to watch your reaction?"

Eve liked that idea even less. "I guess he could have seen the advertisement on TV or in the newspaper and concluded we might be participating, but I don't think he would have been so petty as to pull anything so contrived."

"But did he see you?"

"I thought for a moment he might have, but I turned away."

"Poor sweetie. No wonder you look positively ill." Rae studied her wan face, her own softened by compassion. "You're having regrets, aren't you?"

Eve covered her face with her hands and groaned. "Go ahead and gloat."

"This is too upsetting for that—but there is only one thing to do."

"Which is?"

"We need you doing the same thing."

Just the thought made Eve's stomach roil. "I have no desire to go out with another Wes. Can we table this?"

"I didn't mean that literally, although you may be on to something—look at your reac-

tion to his Sam look-alike. But," she added at
Eve's warning look, "bite the bullet and have
an evening out, Eve. With someone."

"I'm still trying to come to terms with what
an idiot I've been."

"Knowing you, you'll hide in your apartment
and become a hoarder."

"The neighbors might have something to say
regarding the wildlife that would begin seep-
ing from the nooks and crannies," Eve replied.
Droll humor was the best she could do for the
moment. "Would you like to know how we
did money-wise on Friday?"

"I saw on the news that the event broke last
year's total."

Eve rose and hurried to her desk and brought
out her planner, where inside she'd tucked her
report that she'd produced over the weekend.
Retracing her steps, she set the sheet before
Rae.

"Nice job."

Eve gave much of the credit to the athletes, who tirelessly allowed themselves to be dropped into the tank. But she did admit that it took a bit of salesmanship to get a ten-dollar bill out of a customer, instead of just a five, and a twenty instead of a ten—and to have the donor walk away feeling good that they'd done something kind for someone in need.

"How did Honor do?" Rae asked when she was finished.

"Not so well on sales," Eve admitted, acknowledging that Lisa was right. "But Honor is great at anticipating needs, and she was very good with the kids, then invaluable setting up and cleaning up."

"Did she enjoy herself?"

"She seemed to. She was thrilled to get a few autographed photos to take to her kids."

"My dentist is divorced," Rae announced abruptly.

It took Eve a moment to follow that sharp detour off topic. "Rae—stop!"

The next day, Lisa didn't show until almost noon. Then she announced she'd only come in to collect her things and get her last paycheck. While she didn't bear the same attitude she exhibited on Monday, she worked hard to pretend Eve wasn't in the office and didn't say goodbye to anyone. That struck Eve as saddest of all, since she lunched with the other girls daily.

"And I thought I had problems," Honor said, when the front glass entry door shut behind Lisa.

"She's never going to be happy, unless she nabs Prince Harry," Tara replied, with a wry smile. Then she glanced at Honor. "You want to go to lunch with Kristen and me? There's this great salad bar that has the best view of construction workers right now. Tuesdays are our Wicked Fantasy lunches. Can you think of anything to make munching on rabbit food more appetizing?"

Honor looked around to make sure no one was standing behind her chair. "You mean me?"

"Yeah. We would have asked you sooner," Tara admitted, "but Lisa vetoed the idea."

Honor looked at Eve hopefully. "That won't leave you shorthanded handling the phones, will it, Eve?"

"Oh, I think between Rae and I, we can manage. Go and enjoy—but practice safe lunch!"

Laughing, the women took off faster than if the fire alarm had gone off in the building. It was good to see the others be more welcoming to Honor. She was a little older, but she really was a nice woman.

Rae called from her office. "You could do with some fantasizing yourself."

Eve knew she was right, but when she pictured low-slung jeans on a bare-chested man, she couldn't help but want it to be Derek. What was the point of kidding herself? It would be Valentine's Day in a week, and it was still cold, so that view wasn't likely to happen anyway. At least she wouldn't have to pretend to be thrilled this year, as when Wes used to stop at the supermarket on the way home to bring her whatever box of candy was left on the shelves, then ended up eating most of it himself.

"Did you hear me?" Rae called louder.

"Sorry, what?"

"Will you consider meeting the kid brother of my friend? He's new in town and Karyl hopes Kyle will make the move permanent."

"Karyl? That's not a name I'm familiar with." Eve printed the last accounts payable check and brought it to Rae for her signature. "Refresh my memory, and he better not be young enough to be my nephew."

"Karyl is my age, smarty. You're safe." With

a mock warning look, Rae finished ticking details off her fingers. "And Karyl owns the art gallery in Cherry Creek North."

No wonder she didn't recognize the name. She rarely shopped in those high-end stores, although that's where her New Year's dress had come from. "What does the brother do?"

"He was a butler, but his client died and left him part of his fortune. He's taking some time to decide what to do with the rest of his life."

Eve sunk into the chair facing her boss. "Are you serious?"

"Okay, no. But it was worth it to see your face. He's about to retire from the military. He went in young."

"Oh." That was admirable. She took a deep breath. It would take someone of honor and stamina to make her forget Derek. "All right," she said slowly. "I'll try."

With a whoop, Rae ordered her out of her office, then closed the door. When Eve got to her desk, she saw by the lights that Rae was on the phone. Had she made a mistake? It had been a while since she'd seen Rae this excited.

When the light on the phone went out, Eve held her breath waiting to learn what was coming next. A moment later the door to Rae's office opened.

"Eleven-thirty on Valentine's Day at Mocha Canyon."

Eve's heart sank. Not the restaurant where she saw Derek with the Sam look-alike!

"What's wrong?" Rae asked. "Gus has taken me there on a Valentine's Day. They do an outstanding job."

"Okay." But would she be able to swallow a single bite of anything? "It's on my calendar," she said, doing just that. It struck her that her penmanship had never looked more shaky.

Eve was tempted to cancel the date at least once an hour over the next week, but when that day came, she tried to dress with special care. She wore a powder-blue sweater dress that she felt complemented her eyes, and the seed pearl earrings that her parents had given her when she turned twenty-one.

Rae gave her a nod of approval when she saw her, and the others in the office whistled and asked a dozen questions. She admitted nothing except that she did indeed have a lunch date.

"You are such a dark horse," Tara declared with respect. "The first time I saw you, I thought there was no way you'd last a month. You had a good sense of humor, but you acted like you doubted your every move."

"That's because I did," Eve said with a wry smile.

When she slipped on her ivory cape to leave for her lunch date, Rae assured her that if she wanted to take some extra time, she'd earned it.

"Let's just hope that I'm not back in a few

minutes," she replied. "I'm more anxious about this than I was about my first day here."

"And look how that turned out," Rae reminded her. "Now get out—and don't come back unless you're willing to share delicious details."

At the hotel, she handed over her SUV to the valet because she was wearing heels that were gorgeous but difficult to walk in even though there was no more ice or snow in the parking lot. All but sick to her stomach, she entered the lobby and then angled over to the restaurant.

"Good afternoon, miss," the soft-spoken hostess greeted her. "Are you meeting someone?"

"A Mr. Kyle Johnson," Eve said, almost getting tongue-tied because the name didn't feel comfortable to her.

The Asian beauty checked her book and beamed. "Carlo, would you please escort Ms. Easton to Mr. *Johnson's* table."

With a nod the handsome assistant smiled at Eve and beckoned her to accompany him. "Happy Valentine's Day, Ms. Easton," he said. "I hope you enjoy your experience."

"I've heard you do make your holiday lunches special, so I'm sure I will."

Eve had never been inside the place, but she'd heard enough over the past few days to know it should be a treat—if the butterflies in her tummy ever settled down. The restaurant was decorated with the obvious theme of chocolate, the dark chocolate walls adorned with every photo of delectable dessert imaginable between sconces bearing flameless candles. The seating was a mixture of booths and tables with white and gold chairs and café au lait tablecloths and darker napkins. Carlo led her around a center court of booths on the top of which was set a fabulous spray of red roses and a sculpture that included a white-chocolate cupid overseeing the diners. Eve was so transfixed by the culinary artwork that she was slow to realize Carlo had stopped just beneath the cherub.

Her date had spotted her sooner. Wearing a navy blue suit with a red tie in a shade that matched the rose in his hand, he stood.

For a moment she thought she'd confused imagination with reality. With courtly manners, Carlo moved the table a little for her to slide in beside Derek, which she did eagerly and not only because her legs were about to fail her.

As he sat down and set the rose on her gold charger plate, she admitted, "I couldn't picture a face. Whenever I tried, it was always you."

Under the cover of the tablecloth, Derek took her hand in both of his. "I thought once you learned where we were to meet that it would give me away. I thought you'd refuse to come."

Realization made it easier for her to breathe. "So you *knew* I'd seen you that night! Yet you pretended that you didn't. Rotten, G-man. That's groundbreaking heartlessness." But her soft words of rebuke were underscored with lilting laughter, and transfixed by his gaze, she made it evident to him and anyone eavesdropping that she meant none of the censure.

"It was an accident that I went there, but seeing you—that really made an impact. Here," he insisted, lifting her hand to place it over where his heart pounded.

Eve's heart wasn't having any easier a time of things. "Did Rae help you concoct this idea?"

"No, but I had to ask for her cooperation—especially when she admitted she'd been trying to get you to go out with sons, nephews and assorted other relations of friends and business contacts." Searching her face, Derek asked, "Are you going to take that cape off and stay? Are you going to forgive me?"

As humor got the best of her, she did release

the button on the collar. "I suppose you have suffered enough, considering your choice of dates that night."

Although Derek uttered a low epithet, he helped ease the soft material from her shoulders. "You're lovely," he murmured, as a waiter caring for another table, immediately took it and placed it safely on the chair facing them. Derek thanked him and turned back to Eve admitting, "You don't know the half of it."

"Along with the similar looks, would you believe her personality also wasn't that much different than Sam's? That was all Brad's doing. I'd confessed what happened between us, and a few days later, he asked me to take one of his agents to dinner that would be up there. Then he did convince one of his agents, who was a good sport and eager to visit a friend in Boulder, to put a rinse in her hair and come up to pretty much scare me out of five years of my life."

"Oh, no!" Eve said on a gasp. "I owe him a big hug, don't I?"

"Don't even think it," Derek said, his tone almost feral. "I told him that if he ever pulled something like that again, he better buy extra insurance for Sophie."

What Eve was concluding was that they had some extremely caring friends. She reached for the rose and breathed in the delicate scent. "Poor you. Thank you for this."

Visibly heartened, Derek shifted closer so he could keep his voice low. It brought them thigh to thigh, but he didn't make any move to alter that. "Eve…Rae told me that you went back to Texas and returned with a change of heart. She said you missed me. Tell me yourself."

Before Eve could reply, their waiter appeared with a tray bearing two champagne cocktails. After setting them on their charger plates, he asked, "Are we ready to proceed, sir?"

"Please," Derek replied, barely taking his eyes off of her.

As the eager man departed, Derek explained, "I hope you don't mind, there was a special Valentine's Day menu."

"That sounds fun."

He stroked the material at her cuff. "This makes your eyes shimmer like the sea."

"I missed you," Eve said, giving him what he'd asked for. But a lingering hurt forced her to ask, "Why did you move?"

"An unexpected situation came up. A senior agent at my office was being deployed overseas for a few months and was in crisis mode, since he was divorced himself and didn't have anyone close to watch the place. I figured since my lease was nearly up, it fit both of our needs." He slid her a pained look. "I didn't want to experience seeing someone come to pick you up for a date—or worse yet, bring you home at night and not leave."

"I know the feeling," she murmured, thinking of his dinner date.

Derek lifted his glass and waited for her to pick up hers, then he touched the delicate flute to hers. "To new beginnings."

"To fate being patient with fools."

After tasting the bubbling elixir, Derek took hold of her hand again, as though he was half afraid she might still flee. "Yvette at the apartments told me that you'd asked about me."

Surprised, Eve mentally saluted the other woman's sense of fairness. She really couldn't have blamed her if she'd kept that news to herself. "I hated that you thought badly of me. It bothered me more once I went back to Texas and had my eyes seriously opened by my family, loving though they are. Oh!" she added, remembering that he didn't know. "Sela had her daughter. Evagail is eighteen inches, six pounds, eight ounces."

"Congratulate them for me. She sounds like

a cutie, and I know she'll carry her name with dignity as her aunt does hers." Derek entwined his fingers with hers. "Eve…I didn't think badly of you. I was disappointed…and frustrated that you wouldn't give us a chance. I'm the one who behaved badly."

"No." She wouldn't let him take any blame. "Just know that I've missed not seeing you."

"I ached from not seeing you."

Derek began to lean forward to kiss her, but their waiter returned. He placed matching plates with crab cakes in the shape of hearts laying on two asparagus spears that looked like arrows.

"How darling is that?" Eve said, delighted. "I haven't been very hungry lately, but suddenly I'm famished."

"That's a relief, since this was meant to only be a warm-up for tonight," Derek told her.

"That's too much. This is more than wonderful."

"But I want to."

As they took their first taste of food, Eve thought her cup runneth over. At this point, she'd hoped to at least find something she and her "date" had in common.

"You have to tell me where the name Kyle Johnson fits in?" she asked.

"It was an alias I'd used back in the day when I was a field agent."

"That was clever. And is the house you're taking care of far from your office?"

"Maybe five minutes from the apartments. I'm surprised that we didn't pass on the road yet," he added with a wry smile.

"Well, I'm glad for you then. I'd hate for you to have to worry about driving me home and then having to go to the opposite side of the city, especially when it's not the week-end." She would worry about him in inclement weather, too.

"You are probably one of the most consider-
ate people I've ever met."

As sweet as the compliment was, Eve had
to tease him. "Yeah, but we both know that
aside from Ms. Blind Date, you haven't been
getting out much."

"If you undercut yourself again, I'm going
to kiss you breathless, and I won't care how
many people yell, 'Get a room.'"

As tantalizing as that threat—or promise—
was, Eve worried for *his* reputation. "I'll give
you a rain check," she entreated, unabashedly
meeting his intense gaze. "I'll *give* you carte
blanche. You can't risk your job when you
don't know who else is here."

For a moment Derek looked as though he
was going to kiss her anyway. Then with a
heavy sigh, he touched his lips near her ear
and murmured, "Woman, you take my breath
away."

The rest of their lunch passed in a blur for

Eve. She was sure that the filet mignon entrée and the heart-shaped strawberry-cheese tart were delicious, but almost every cell in her being was fixated on Derek, so she had no memory recall of anything else.

When it was time to return to the office, he walked her to her SUV that the valet brought forward. After tipping the young man, Derek signaled that he would get her door.

"Will six-thirty be okay?" he asked her. "Our reservation is for seven."

"Too early," she said, emphatically shaking her head. "It'll take me an hour just to do my hair."

He grinned, but his kiss was anything but humorous. "Don't make me call my secret weapon to send you home early."

"I'll be ready," she promised.

She was ready and at the window when Derek arrived several minutes late. There had been an urgent conference call at the last minute, then traffic had been one big snarl-up getting home. He'd barely had time for a shower and to change into a gray suit, and had risked a ticket racing to Eve's building—not that he was likely to get one once he flashed his ID. But seeing her watching for him at the window brought a smile of pleasure to his lips as he jogged up the sidewalk, his gray trench coat flapping behind him. He completely forgot the afternoon's aggravations and work-related minutiae, especially when she opened the door and he saw what she was wearing.

He tilted his head back and said to the heavens, "Thank you." She had chosen her New Year's dress, the one that left her exquisite back bare and made him wonder for days afterward about what, if anything, she could be wearing beneath it.

"Is it overkill?" she asked with a look of

doubt. "It won't take me two minutes to change."

"Don't you dare. Seeing you in that again was *my* fantasy. Although you are going to need another minute or two," Derek added, stepping inside and shutting the door behind himself to protect her from the cold.

Bemused, she asked, "Because…?"

"I've been dying to do this, and your lip gloss is going to need replacing." With that said, he took her into his arms, brought her unapologetically flush against his body, then kissed her as though it had been months, not weeks since he'd last done so. As far as Derek was concerned, an hour was starting to be too long.

She was like a rare cognac going quickly to his head and he tangled his tongue with hers over and over seeking to imbibe every essence of her. It thrilled him that she kissed him back with equal eagerness, but what had him groaning and growing hard, was sliding his hand down her naked back and then over her sleek bottom.

"Give me strength," he muttered. "Do you have on anything under that?"

Laughing throatily, Eve backed away from his arousal, but not so far that she couldn't wipe her lip gloss from his lower lip. "Don't ask questions that you can't handle the answer to."

She vanished into her bedroom, and then the bathroom. When she returned, she was carrying a matching cashmere shawl that he hadn't seen on the night of the Grainger party, and a bejeweled purse. Her makeup was perfect again, although her lips were slightly more swollen than before. Totally approving of the change and his mark on her, he took the shawl from her and helped wrap her in it.

"Are you sure you're going to be warm enough?" he asked, aching to pull her back into his arms so that she could feel his heart pound and his body swell. For her.

"It's not far to your SUV, or probably not much different to the inside of the restaurant, is it? Unless we're headed toward garden or rooftop dining."

Unable to resist, he touched his lips to the back of her elegant neck. "Close, but not quite."

The restaurant was actually in a stone house, with an atrium center. It was one of the city's better kept secrets and they didn't advertise for the simple reason they didn't need to. They maintained a select clientele and reservations could be at a premium. Derek had been introduced to the owner by his predecessor, and on his other two visits here, he'd spotted a former president, a current senator and at least two billionaires.

"I always thought this was a private residence," Eve said, just before a valet came to open her door.

"Believe it or not, it is. Sebastian has worked for a European head of state, but made his real money catering to the wealthy oil people in Saudi Arabia. Now he can afford to pick his hours and for whom he cooks."

As soon as they entered the candlelit foyer, Derek was greeted warmly by a middle-aged man in an impeccably tailored black suit. "Special Agent-in-Charge Roland, we're so pleased you and your guest are joining us tonight. Everything is prepared."

"Thank you, Maurice. This is Eve Easton," he added, slipping off his coat.

"A pleasure, mademoiselle." Maurice took the coat and handed it silently to a young woman who materialized out of the shadows. "I would recommend you keep your lovely shawl, Ms. Easton, as the rooms are kept comfortable, but you have window seating."

"Thank you for that advice," she murmured.

As the maître d' led the way to their table,

Eve glanced bemusedly at Derek. "This is really where Jimmy Hoffa is hiding, isn't it?" she whispered.

Derek understood her reaction. The restaurant was all about intimacy and the black walls and low lighting assured it. The smells emanating from the kitchen allowed them to forget they'd had a three-course meal only six hours ago. Their table was by the wall-to-wall windows looking out into an atrium garden that included a series of lit chimineas and a tall flowing fountain illuminated by soft lighting. Each table was adorned by candlelight and flowers, and the color theme was a romantic and ethereal white on white.

When their watchful but gracious host left them—without a menu—Eve leaned across the table. "What's next? Does the chef come out with tonight's specials written on his cleaver? Ooh, that would be too *Sweeny Todd*-ish."

"Not exactly, but you're starting to catch on.

There are no menus. When you call, if you can be accommodated, you're told what Sebastian is preparing for the night. You *are* given wine options from his impressive cellar inventory."

"That's generous of him." She glanced around the small, narrow space. "They gave us the entire room."

"It's actually a hallway. I confided my hopes to Maurice to have as much privacy with you as possible. He's a romantic at heart, as you can see. If you'll look through the other windows, you'll see there are several other rooms with various amounts of seating."

"So there's a Mrs. Maurice."

"There is. Sebastian."

If Derek thought he would surprise her, he was wrong. She'd already experienced enough from her time with Rae Grainger that the world was as diverse as it was colorful and complicated.

"His accent would turn anyone gay. I don't

think I'll be practicing my cowgirl French to-night."

Derek had to work on not bursting into laughter. "If it's anything like your singing voice, I hope you'll change your mind. In the meantime…"

He reached into his pocket and brought out a slender black satin box and set it before her. It was difficult to see in the dim lighting, so he wasn't surprised when she blinked at it.

When Eve opened it, saw that it contained a gold bracelet of delicate weaving with blue topaz stones, her hands began to shake. "It's too much," she whispered.

"It's you. At least I think the stones are a perfect match to your eyes."

With an incredulous shake of her head, Eve held it out to him. "Will you put it on me?"

He did and she admired it with quiet wonder. An odd little expression crossed her face, then she reached for her purse. "My gift is far more modest." She drew out a package wrapped in tissue the color of her dress.

Having expected nothing, Derek was taken by surprise for the first time since…he couldn't remember. But it was his eagerness that surprised him. "Would this be a good time to tell you that except for the office Christmas gift exchange, this is the first present that I've received in—I can't remember."

Hearing that, Eve began to try to take it back. "You should let me get you something better."

"There is nothing better," he said, staring at the photo in the silver frame. It had been taken from behind by—it must have been Sophie— at the Neville family cabin. It was when they sat before the fire and didn't realize that anyone was watching. Lost in each other's eyes, their gazes reflected wonder and, yes, the first whispering indications of love.

"She emailed that to me before they flew home," Eve told him.

"It's going on my desk."

"You don't have to," she began.

Her modesty was enchanting, as the photo. "Are you kidding? I want another for the house."

A waiter about half the age of Maurice brought the wine. After the usual formalities, "Lozario" departed, Derek raised his glass to Eve and murmured tenderly. "Hello, you."

"Hi, G-man."

They sipped the vintage Cabernet that he thought was almost as smooth as Eve's kisses, which was exactly what he needed to contain his growing hunger for her.

"So how was Rae once you got back to the office?"

"Smug. All but unbearable." Eve tried not to laugh, but her sparkling eyes gave away her pleasure and appreciation for such concern and friendship. "I'll never be able to leave her now. Even so, she's all but demanding that I go under contract."

"There are worse things. She's opened doors for you, but she also wants to protect you. I would dare to say that she loves you."

Their first course arrived, pan-seared scallops and warm spinach salad. Every bite melted in their mouths. Conversation flowed just as easily now that doubt and the past were no longer roadblocks to what was blossoming between them.

The second course was a spicy Bloody Mary consommé served in twenty-four-karat-gold-clad demitasse cups. Then came duck with winter squash and mushrooms, enhanced with a touch of blood orange.

"The last time I had duck was in New Orleans and they put capers in it," Eve said. "I thought I'd never eat it again, but this is heavenly."

Nevertheless, the dessert topped the meal—a

cherry flambé. "Let me just say that this definitely beats thirty candles destroying a cup-
cake," Eve mused, as Lozario extinguished
the flames and served them.

As wonderful as dinner was, Derek couldn't
deny that what he savored most was the moment they were alone again in his vehicle. The
valet had already turned on the heater and seat
warmers, and he enjoyed watching Eve snuggle deeper into the luxurious leather.

It was barely past ten o'clock, but traffic had
thinned significantly. "Do you have a heavy
day tomorrow?" he asked, already strategiz-
ing. One way or another, he didn't plan to wait
until the weekend to see her again.

"No, but Thursday through Saturday evening will be nonstop. How about you?"

"Better than that," he said, knowing he
couldn't explain investigations and endless
threats. "Otherwise, I'll mostly be waiting for
a certain someone to tell me that she's not too

tired to see me tomorrow, otherwise, Sunday is too damned long to wait."

"Maybe even Saturday night if you can stay awake that long."

Hope was an eagle about to burst through his ribs. "Sweetheart, if you call, I'm coming."

They'd reached her apartment and he put his trench coat over her shoulders, then kept his arm around her all the way up the sidewalk. While there was no new snow, and he knew that she wasn't going to complain about the cold, he needed any physical contact he could get to keep assuring him that there was a to-morrow for them. This new atmosphere, or understanding between them still seemed too new, too fragile to be true.

At the door, when she turned to him, he didn't hesitate to fold her into his arms. But it cost him to control his need and hunger. "So tonight was a success?" he asked gruffly, after a first, languid kiss.

"The best."

"I hate for it to end, but I know you need to get to bed." When she reached up to silence him with her fingertips, he took hold of them and kissed each one. "It's all right, sweetheart. You're worth waiting for."

"You don't have to," she murmured. "Don't go."

Chapter Seven

Eve understood when Derek stiffened and was hesitant to react. Despite the wonderful time they'd had tonight—today—her track record with risk taking in the commitment department didn't inspire full confidence yet, and here she was offering him one of the biggest gifts a woman could to a man. Herself.

His gaze was searching, even intense as he tried to read her deepest thoughts. "I can't tell you what hearing that does to me," he told her. "But you don't have to do this. I appreciate what getting to this point has meant to you."

How to convince him that her invitation wasn't based on some archaic sense of sacrifice or obligation? Then the old saying, "a picture is worth a thousand words" came to mind. That held merit in this instance, too, she thought. So deciding she would show him, she unlocked her door and took his hand to lead him inside.

Oddly enough, as she began to lock up, Derek still stopped her.

"Eve...I don't have anything with me. I wanted you to understand that we can be on your timetable."

She finished securing the dead bolt. Her timetable...when was the last time she thought she had a use for one?

As her thoughts raced from humorous to flirtatious, she could barely keep a wicked gleam out of her eyes. "I'm so out of practice," she began, removing his coat from around her shoulders, and her shawl. She placed both on a nearby chair, along with her purse. Turning back to him, she stroked her hand along his tie, feeling the strong beat of his heart. "I'm torn between blushing and laughing. You see, Rae gave us stockings for Christmas along with our bonuses, and she was *really* bad with mine, if you catch my drift." When Derek simply kept watching her, she added, "As in *naughty?*"

As his eyes lit with amusement, he took hold of her hand with his, and pressed a kiss into her palm. "Are you saying that you won't have trouble finding me in the dark?"

"There's an assortment," Eve acknowledged. "I think there's even something that looks like a sea urchin. I was so intrigued, I almost opened the packaging to see."

His chest shook with laughter as he took her completely into his arms and let her *feel* how this subject was gaining more and more of his interest. "In case you haven't noticed yet, I'd love to be your lab experiment."

This time when he kissed her, Eve let her heart have full reign over her passion. Whatever the future held, she would trust in Derek. She'd backed up from and sidestepped life for the last time.

As he stroked his hands down her bare back, she sighed with pleasure. "How can you be that warm when we've just been in below-freezing air?"

"Probably because I've been fantasizing about having you this close again since New Year's. God, Eve, you feel so good."

"So do you." With her arms around his neck and standing on tiptoe, she pressed herself against him. "But you're wearing too many clothes."

"Complaints, complaints," he said against her lips. "I'm done arguing with you."

The only substantial light came from a stained-glass lamp by the front window. A fainter glow from the bedroom was actually the bathroom nightlight. As Eve took hold of his tie and provocatively led him in that direction, she asked, "Would you like something to drink?"

"Uh-huh. Nectar of Eve."

As a subtle shiver of excitement swept through her, Eve wondered if what she'd thought of as his seriousness all this time was long-repressed passion. Although she suspected Derek was always on the FBI clock in some way, until this moment, he had only let her see flickers of the depth of his sexual appetite. How could Samantha have turned away from this man? Eve wasn't even sure she could satisfy the hunger she saw in his gaze, and she began to slip her arms around his waist, wanting the reassurance of a hug, but he caught her by the wrists before she succeeded.

"Sweetheart, I have some paraphernalia I have to get off."

Her fingers had brushed against some of it,

and she pointed to the bathroom behind him, thinking it sweet how he was trying to protect her from being overwhelmed with that side of his life. "Help yourself. Um…the other paraphernalia is in the bottom left drawer."

He kissed her briefly and went in there, shutting the door behind him.

Eve looked around. Now what? In the movies, women stripped fast or at least to the bare minimum, and crawled into bed positioning themselves provocatively. She thought Michelle Pfeiffer was everywoman as she prepared herself for Al Pacino in *Frankie and Johnny.* But Eve's dress had cost at least twenty times more than what Frankie had been wearing. Add that a hangnail could render it as useless as anything but a costly dust rag, she went to the closet and gently eased it off, slipping out of her four-inch heels at the same time. She was glad for the privacy to remove the modesty petals the dress required. Only a

B cup, technically she didn't need a bra, but her nipples made it mandatory because even in a sheer bra, the "girls" had a mind of their own and always acted like puppies begging for attention.

About to slip off her lace-and-satin thong panties, which were the only kind she could wear without the dress revealing them, the bathroom door opened. All reflexes, she spun around.

"Dear God," Derek murmured.

Eve knew it was too late to cross her arms and attempt modesty, besides, she was too fascinated in seeing him with the towel around his waist. He was as toned as she'd discerned from the times being in his arms and being crushed into snow had suggested. But this visual introduction was a turn-on. As he crossed to her, she couldn't miss that he was turned on, too. Still. Okay, she amended feeling her latest blush, more.

When he reached her, he simply took hold of her waist and lifted her as he would a doll, until he could take her right nipple into his mouth. When he lathed her with his tongue, Eve thought she could orgasm there and then. As the world spun, she gripped his rock-hard shoulders and wrapped her legs around his trim waist. Closing her eyes, she arched her back letting the sensations course like a thousand needles from her breast to her womb. He performed the same wet and hot ministrations on her left breast, then clasped her against him and took her mouth for a deep tongue-delving kiss.

The next thing she knew, she was being lowered onto the bed and he was covering her with his body. "You're perfect," he rasped, as he stroked her from her neck to that lace waistband. "I knew you would be."

"I'm short, but all muscle," she mused. "You picked me up like I was a cake box."

"And you're sweeter," he said, scoring a trail all over her torso with his mouth. "I thought I'd died and gone to heaven when I saw this."

His teeth took hold of the lace of her panties as his thumbs traced the rest of it down to her core. The sensations had Eve digging her heels into the mattress, but whether to escape too much of a good thing, or to offer herself for everything, she couldn't say.

But he knew. Derek rubbed his cheek against the satin triangle, then gently grazed her thigh with his teeth. "You're like a little wild thing that has been locked up and denied petting for too long," he said, his voice a soft rumble. "Pleasure has almost become pain, hasn't it?"

"Yes."

"Not after tonight. By the time we're done, you're going to know you were born for my hands, and my mouth. My body. And I'll feel the same way. I want you like I've never wanted anything or anyone in my life." To press the point home, he opened his mouth over that small triangle of satin.

"Derek…please."

"I will," he said, shifting to ease the lace down her hips and legs. "I used to watch you," he said, his voice as soothing as his caress. "You were as dainty as any of the flowers in your yard. I envied the man who could put that smile of pleasure on you as you lifted your face to the sun."

"It wasn't a man. It was the solace of nature on a troubled heart."

"I know…now. But if I die trying, I'm going to be the cause of all your future smiles."

Like now as he began to taste her. Eve found that he was intent on making her as comfortable and ready for him as he could. Her mouth went dry. He hadn't used the most outrageous gift from Rae's condom basket, which was probably a good thing. Regardless, his possession was going to be a force to be reckoned with.

She learned what it was like to be savored like spring's first fruit after the hardest winter. She couldn't help the tears that seeped from behind her tightly closed lids, or the keening cry when he led her to her first sharp climax.

"I'm sorry," she said between ragged breaths.

Derek kissed his way up her body, until he covered her with his. "For what, sweetness? For letting me see that I turn you on as much as you do me? You can buy a performance anywhere," he said, beginning to probe the first sensitive folds where she continued to pulsate. "I want your helpless honesty and hunger. I want your heart. Kiss me," he rasped, locking his mouth to hers.

She did, and gave him what else he wanted, what she needed, and clung to him as he began his slow invasion. His tongue matched the patient, tentative thrusts, the twin invasions raising the temperatures of their bodies higher and higher, until their skin was slick. But that only made every caress more sensual and tantalizing.

When she lightly scraped her short nails over his nipple, Derek groaned with pleasure and rolled her over to bring her on top of him. "Do that with your teeth."

Eve did, then soothed him with her tongue and suckled.

With a guttural expletive, Derek filled his hand with her short hair and drew her up for a ravenous kiss. In the next instant, he rolled her beneath him and cupped her bottom to bring her closer as he drove deeper and deeper.

"I thought I could wait," he said, his voice almost sounding raw as the pressure built to the impossible. "But I've wanted you for too long."

Eve arched off the bed, then wrapped her legs around his waist as desperately as her arms clung to his broad, tense shoulders. She couldn't get close enough, even though she felt like she might burn up or shatter into a thousand pieces.

It was Derek's last ravenous kiss, his urgent thrusts that made the promise of ecstasy a reality, lifting them to that blessed summit. They drank each other's wordless cries, entwined as one.

Later, when Derek lay on his back, with Eve tucked against him, he stared at the ceiling, pondering all that had happened and what he was feeling. Not just about what they'd just shared, but how it refined everything that they'd experienced since New Year's Eve. His heart was full. But he knew what a fragile feeling that was. He could still lose her, lose everything he really wanted.

For her part, Eve was tracing a path with her fingers through his chest hair. Her delicate touch was almost ticklish, and he took hold of her hand to give a warning nip to her fingertips.

"That's a shortcut to getting even less sleep tonight," he warned.

She laughed softly and rolled onto her tummy, to meet his narrow-eyed gaze. "Ask me if I care?" Then her expression softened and she laid her cheek on his chest. "Thank you for being so careful with me."

Derek grunted. "Not careful enough."

"I'm not sore."

The way his body was reacting to her talented hands, she would be. But he repressed those needs as much as he was able because there was something that needed to be done first. "We need to talk."

The serenity and joy in her eyes was replaced with curiosity, then fear. "Derek—no. Don't tell me if it's about something at the Bureau. Not tonight."

"It isn't. It's about us."

Relaxing again, she teased, "Okay, so is this where you tell me that you were in lust with me from the moment you moved in next door? Under the circumstances, I forgive you."

"Close."

Eve raised her head and searched his eyes. "I was joking."

"I'm not. Shortly after we became neighbors, I stopped—being a husband to Sam." Although he saw shock, then questions in Eve's lovely eyes, he was impressed that she said nothing, waiting on him to finish. Then again, he understood her unwillingness to accelerate her own pain, maybe even anger. "Sam had a history of being untrustworthy. We should have called it quits before I got the Texas assignment, but I knew she could have harmed my career with lies and accusations if I filed for divorce, and I chose—in hindsight foolishly—not to take that gamble. But I made it clear that I had no interest or intent in ever having sex with her again."

Gasping, Eve sat up. *"Derek."*

"Well, hell, I didn't want to find out six months or a year down the road that I was contaminated with something." He could see she was drawing some conclusions and beginning to struggle with them. Derek couldn't help but to stroke her thigh to soothe her. "Sweetheart, I never believed that she would fish so close to home." At her doubtful look, he swore. "Damn it, I did not. And I sure as hell couldn't make myself believe a man would betray a woman like you."

"How long did it take before you realized she chose Wes?"

The barely audible question was like a fist squeezing the blood from his heart. "The day I came to confront him. You knew when you opened the door to me."

"Yes. No. Well...you looked so angry. You

were always somber. Serious. But what I saw in your eyes chilled me to the core."

When she shivered from just the memory, Derek rose on his elbow and reached over to get the glass of wine she'd gotten for them before they'd started talking. "Take a sip." As she did, he continued with gruff tenderness, "I was furious—scared to death that through her selfishness and carelessness that she'd somehow infected you." At her startled look, he added bitterly, "There was no reason for me to trust that Wes was the only one. I forced her to get checked out by threatening to report Wes to the district's superintendent. You deserved more than to be free of Wes, you deserved to know that you were healthy."

Her hand started shaking, and she had to hand him back the glass. "It never crossed my mind to check, not once I knew it was her. Anyone else, I would have had some testing done myself."

Now would come the fury, Derek thought with increasing dread. Her mind would start looking back and seeing his share of guilt in all this. Having known what Sam was, why hadn't he warned her that Sam didn't see a wedding ring as a boundary? He was half tempted to slide his hand to Eve's nape and draw her to him for a kiss that would delay what he feared most. Maybe he could love her well enough to win himself a modicum of forgiveness for his collusion. However, she deserved better than that. She deserved his honesty.

"The other reason that I was scared sick for you was because I fell."

Eve frowned and shook her head. She clearly wasn't going to let herself go there.

"Yes. I fell for you. You made fun of me when I told you how I watched you with Elvis and our elderly neighbors, but I did. I also watched you swim in your pool, all grace and ease like the water was your true home. When you'd climb out deliciously wet, your suit more like a second skin than that gorgeous dress you wore on New Year's, I headed straight for a cold shower." Derek closed his eyes, starting to ache anew with those bittersweet memories. "I started dreaming about you and living in fear that I'd say your name in my sleep."

"Did you know I'd moved up here?" she asked, with dread. "Is that why you took this post?"

He shook his head adamantly. "No. I swear it. I wanted to ask, but I thought it was only fair punishment to deny myself that information." She had looked so shattered and humiliated the last time he'd seen her. He'd imagined a scenario where, given some time, he could look her up again. And then he'd reluctantly accepted the invitation to a party that changed his life forever—or might finish destroying it. He laid back against the pillows and rubbed his face with both hands wishing he'd made different choices. Wishing…

"I'm glad I never knew that I had my own flesh-and-blood guardian angel." Eve spoke as though caught in a dream. "We might have ended up betraying our spouses as badly as they did us."

"You're not angry? Hurt?"

"I was, but it was making me sick. I had to let it go." Eve met his gaze without hesitation. "You see, Wes didn't touch me for almost a year before the divorce. I asked that we go to counseling. He refused and insisted he was just having some stress at school and that I should quit acting like a needy, spoiled juvenile and think of him for once.

"I started visiting my family more, hoping the old adage of distance making the heart grow fonder would work, although now I don't know why. That last insult changed something in me." She stroked her fingers over his chest, her gaze following the patterns she made. "My brother Nicholas blew a gasket when he saw me just before everything went crazy. I'd gotten physically ill, and to convince him that it wasn't morning sickness, but more likely the beginnings of an ulcer, I had to confess the state of my marriage. He suggested something that probably helped put that look on my face that you saw that day. He said, 'If he doesn't want you, Evie, he's screwing someone else and you need to prepare yourself for the possibility that your competition might not be your own sex.' Later that afternoon when I arrived home, you came pounding on our door."

The heavens had smiled on him. Them. Derek closed his eyes briefly, savoring the joy that followed relief. Then he reached for her. "Come here, little mermaid, I need to kiss you."

Although she murmured, "Me, too," she resisted his coaxing, only to continue her caresses, her mouth following the whispery soft journey of her fingers—lower, and lower.

Derek's abdomen tightened reflexively from tension and hope. When her cheek brushed against his already full erection, he sucked in his breath on an exquisite stab of desire. When she repeated that caress with her lips, it was all he could do not to drag her beneath him, and bury himself deeper than he had the first time, and he wouldn't give a damn if there was no time to open one of the foil packets he'd gotten from the bathroom when she'd gone for the wine. If he got her pregnant, she would have to marry him, and then she would be his forever.

"Eve." The hand he stretched to stroke her hair was unsteady. She was killing him…with pleasure.

"I don't have words," she whispered against him. "You saved me, and then nobly walked away."

"Not so nobly."

"My G-man."

Derek stopped thinking then. He simply gave himself up to the woman who now owned his soul.

"You know I love you, don't you?" Eve asked. "But let me repeat—if you ever pull a stunt like the Kyle Johnson episode, I'm out of here."

Rae laughed, fully relishing her part in the plan. "I take it that last night was as good as lunch? Of course it was, I've never seen you look better. A bit sleepy-eyed maybe," she added with a mischievous look from under her mascara-thick lashes.

And a bit achy, Eve thought easing onto the chair in Rae's office; but it was a good kind of ache. "Thank you, but walking into that restaurant cost me most of what little confidence and courage I've regained since my marriage and divorce."

"Enough about the past. Tell me that Derek proposed?" Rae said, eagerly leaning forward.

"No, of course not."

"Demure looks charming on you, but don't tell me that you can't finally see the man loves you?"

Yes, Eve thought, her heart all but threatening to pound its way through her ribs, she did. But he hadn't said the words yet. Technically, she amended, with a secret thrill as she remembered his confession about "falling." "But it's so soon. Why can't we just enjoy this—awakening?" she asked with a wistful smile.

Rae grimaced, but said with respect, "You'll make a good agent's wife. You're very discreet." She slid a folder to her. "These are my notes on a meeting I had with the board of the Denver Movie Festival. We have the contract for this summer's gala."

If Eve hadn't spent last night with the most romantic man on the planet, she would have been speechless, but this was a huge deal, too. "Oh, my—congratulations!" She picked up the folder with new respect for her boss. "I thought they book their planning people a year in advance?"

"They do, but they've already caught the company they'd hired first padding their invoices, and they're threatening to sue if they're not released from their contract. As you can imagine, no one needs that kind of publicity, and they were awarded it, albeit reluctantly."

As Eve quickly scanned Rae's notes, she almost choked on the budget and the festival's dates. "Can we make this happen? Don't we have half the size staff as the other company has?"

"Yes, but what we have is integrity and heart."

"I will get on this right away. Is it all right if I pass Thursday's venue to Tara? It's all set except for the last-minute calls, especially about the perishable items. I'll still oversee every-thing myself that evening."

"Then I have no problem with that," Rae re-plied. "But something you'll want to keep in mind is that it's entirely likely that some mem-bers of the D.M.F. board will be there."

That wasn't anything new. Half of their client list came to them after having been to one of their previous events. But it was Rae's job as overseer to remind her—and the rest of the staff—to feel as though they were "on camera" every second.

Eve collected the rest of her things and rose, "I'd better get to it."

"Sorry if this interferes with any lunch plans with you-know-who."

"No lunch plans," she replied with a blissful smile. "We're having dinner instead."

That evening, Eve had to delay meeting with Derek, but by dusk, she made it into the apartment's parking lot where he was waiting in his SUV. When she signaled that she was ready, he led the way to the house that he was residing in while the other agent was overseas. He'd told her over breakfast that morning that he would like her to know how to get there and offered dinner as added incentive. Eve didn't need any incentive, and she'd laughed and blushed when he added, "You might appreciate the thicker walls by the time I'm done making love to you in all of the ways I have in my dreams."

As he'd previously explained, the house was only a few minutes away and fairly easy to find. It was a quaint cottage that had once been a caretaker's house on a larger estate. The estate was now subdivided into gentleman ranches—properties of twenty to fifty acres, most hosting contemporary-style structures. Being nestled amid a small cove of evergreens, the stone dwelling was spared that visual and instantly transported one into another time.

"No wonder your agent wanted someone re-liable to keep an eye on things," Eve said, instantly enchanted, as she exited her SUV. "It's so romantic."

"Ben has been renovating the place since buying it." Derek took her small suitcase from her that she'd packed this morning after they'd made their plans. "He's redone all of the wir-ing, replaced the carpeting with hardwood floors and upgraded the bathrooms."

The house was small—only two bedrooms, a cozy living room with a stone fireplace and a kitchen. But the kitchen was the same size as the living room, leaving space for the pedestal wood dinette table and four chairs. It looked like the kitchen cabinets had been replaced in the past few years, and the counters were a black-and-tan granite.

"Ben has nice taste," Eve said, as she made

a slow three-sixty turn. She admired the buttery-white textured walls that kept the place from being too dark, situated under the trees as it was. The masculine touches were in the choice of the brown leather couch and recliner, and the simple but sturdy coffee and side tables. She found creativity and humor in a bowl of water-polished riverbed rocks set in the center of the coffee table. Balanced on it was a piece of driftwood that, from where she was standing, looked like a bull-rider on a mighty Brahma.

"He's a weekend carpenter," Derek explained. "He made the tables, including the one in the kitchen. The tools in his workshop, which was originally the unattached garage, are just about all that survived his divorce."

"This is so much nicer for you than the apartment," she said, taking in the view from each window. It reminded her of the Graingers' mountain home, without the mountains. "After a stressful day, this will do you more good than being a cave dweller." At Derek's short laugh, she shrugged. "That's what my father called my apartment when I told him where I'd moved once I got up here. He was just furious that I had to give up the house."

Having locked up and setting her case by the hallway, Derek shrugged out of his jacket and came to ease her into his arms. "You're the only stress relief that works for me."

His kiss was cherishing, yet hungry, and Eve wrapped her arms around his neck, eager for her taste of the man who had threatened—despite her heavier schedule—to claim most of her concentration during the day. She moaned with pleasure as he slid his hands inside her coat and blazer to caress her breasts, teasing her nipples that quickly tightened.

"I feel lace," he murmured against her lips.

"You feel more than that." As another delicious current of sensation rushed through her, she sighed. "G-man, what you do to me."

"That works both ways."

This time his kiss was a little more intense and he slid his hands to her hips where he lifted her to cup his arousal. "Home, sweet home."

Laughing softly, Eve slid her hands down his shoulders, loving his powerful body. But when she began to wrap her arms around his waist, he grunted and released her to tug off his gun, BlackBerry, extra clips and badge. "Let me put these up," he said, withdrawing to the bedroom.

Watching him take her case on the way, Eve took off her coat and laid it with his, then she slid off her red blazer, which left her in a V-necked white blouse and black pencil skirt. Returning to the kitchen, she admired the bouquet of daffodils in the tall drinking glass on the center of the table.

"Pretty touch," she said, hearing Derek return. "Something smells good, too. What time did you leave the office to do all this? Noon?" She also didn't think he would have worn jeans or skipped a tie if he'd come straight from the office.

"Three."

"You know, you don't have to hide your gun and things from me the minute you're around me. What you do is important. It's a large part of who you are. It may still intimidate me, probably scare me if I let myself dwell on it too long, but I get it. I'll get used to it."

"That's all I'm doing," he said, wrapping his arms around her from behind and sliding his hands down her tummy to her womb and lower, then pressing himself against her again. "Getting you used to it."

The way he was stroking her made her ache and grow weak and moist. She reached back for him, wanting his mouth, and he gave it to her, and the tongue-tangling kiss that had her helplessly, instinctively grinding her hips against him.

"Damn, I wanted to do this right," he groaned against the side of her neck. "At least pour you a glass of wine."

But as he began tugging her skirt up over her hips, Eve said, "You're doing it right."

Turning to face him, she wasn't exactly patient with his shirt buttons. Then she nuzzled in the smattering of hair and breathed in his scent. When she licked at the first hint of dampness on his skin, the sound that rose from his throat was almost feral.

"The only thing better than feeling your hands on me is your sweet little mouth."

"You're working out more than you used to," she noted, painstakingly exploring the delineation of each muscle. "You were always toned, but now..."

"It helps keep my mind off things." When

she wet him with her tongue, he sucked in his breath and exhaled on an expletive.

"Things like that?"

"Exactly," Derek muttered, reaching into his pocket.

When he pulled out a foil packet, Eve started unfastening his belt. "Special Agent Prepared," she said with a cheeky grin. By the time he had the packet open, she had his jeans open. "Give it to me."

He did, but the second she went to work, he groaned. "That may have been too good of an idea. Step out," he rasped.

"Huh?"

"Your panties."

She had been so transfixed on him that she hadn't realized that as he'd been caressing her, he'd sent them to the floor. She stepped out of them and her heels at the same time.

The second she did, Derek had her in his arms and kicked a chair away from the table.

As he sat down, and lowered her onto him, he was breathing as though he'd just run a whole series of sprints. "I hope you're wet enough."

"I am."

But in the next instant, he froze and swore. "Not. Sweetheart, I'm sorry."

The discomfort was brief, and Eve easily overcame it as she covered his face with feathering kisses while shifting and rocking on his lap. A sensual roll one way, a subtle shimmy another, and she could accept all of him.

Whispering his adoration and approval, Derek framed her face with his hands and kissed her deeply. At the same time, he unbuttoned her silk blouse and the front closure of her lacy bra. Aided by the sweep of his hands to cup and caress her breasts, they slid off her shoulders. As Eve arched her back to give him better access, her things glided the rest of the way to the floor.

"Farther," Derek said, bracing her back with

his left forearm. With his right, he stroked her from throat to where they were joined. As he found the little nub, he took her right breast into his mouth.

Eve couldn't have controlled her body if she wanted to. The timeless need to find release from the building energy inside her set the rhythm as she rode him.

"Hold me," he rasped.

She did, which freed his hands to grip her hips to help her. Lifting her, he then drove her down, and himself deeper. She wanted to kiss him, but there wasn't enough air and she could only fill her hands with his hair and press her forehead to his to watch it happen for both of them.

Only when they were on the slow descent did she seek that kiss, and the sensual plumbing triggered a gratifying second wave of ecstasy. Derek crushed her to his pounding heart and whispered her name like a prayer.

Finally, when she could speak, Eve laid her head against his shoulder and tasted the salty moisture on his neck. "If that was the appetizer, I can't wait for the main course."

Derek groaned. "I've probably ruined that pork loin in the oven." But he kept stroking her bare back and caressing her bottom. Continued to gently nibble on her earlobe and brush his lips along her jaw line. "I keep hoping I'm not going to break you in two. Once I feel your hands on me, I can't think straight."

He reached to the floor and picked up her things. He tossed both items on the table, and then twisted out of his shirt, only to help her into it. It was way too large, but from the way his possessive gaze made her feel as he also unfastened her skirt and helped her out of it, it was perfect.

"That's all you need," he said, stroking her once more before only securing the middle button. "I want to be able to get at you when the urge hits."

Which it did only minutes after finally feeding her.

On Thursday, Derek didn't get to see Eve as they'd planned, as her event turned into something of a nightmare when a bus careened out of control and ran into the building that she and her team were in. He'd wanted to drive straight down there, but she'd assured him that they'd been on the opposite side of the lobby and that traffic was already a nightmare. Even so, he pressed her to call him the moment she was on her way home, which was after midnight. Then again when she was locked safely in her apartment. That conversation turned into some stimulating foreplay and left him aching for her despite the relief he sought afterward in the shower.

On Friday, a special meeting was called for

senior management of several area law enforcement agencies, forcing Derek to get down to Boulder. Eve was tied up again anyway, but on Saturday evening, he was still in Boulder.

It was Sunday before he returned to Denver—with a mild case of food poisoning.

"Derek, how awful," Eve said when he called her from the house. "I'll come nurse you. You'll need to stay hydrated, and do you have crackers? I'll make you toast and potato soup."

Derek wouldn't hear of it. "I make a crappy patient," he said. "You don't need to find that out yet."

"I don't believe that."

Despite feeling like road kill, her soft laugh left him longing for her. He loved how often she laughed now. He was responsible for that change in her. That filled him with as much pride and pleasure as did the way she sexually responded to him.

"Tell me about your day," he coaxed. "Better yet, tell me what you're wearing."

It was Wednesday before the world turned right-side up again—at least schedule-wise. It had been a whole week since they'd seen each other and enough was enough as far as Eve was concerned. Upon leaving a dinner meeting with the film festival people that Rae had asked her to accompany her to, she made a brief stop and then triggered Derek's number on her cell phone.

From the sound of his slightly muffled voice, Eve experienced a pang of guilt. "Did I wake you?"

"I was almost dozing off. But you know that doesn't matter."

"Guess who's two miles from you with a bottle of Pinot Noir?"

Derek was immediately concerned due to the latest snowstorm. "What are you doing driving farther in the weather than you need to? You should have gone straight home. I'd have come to you."

"Okay," she said on a sigh. "If you want me to try to find a safe spot to turn around—"

"Get over here. But be careful, damn it."

He was watching for her and strode to the door of her SUV to sweep her into his arms and carry her inside. Slamming the front door shut behind him, he let her slide down his body, clearly enjoying any and every bit of contact he could squeeze out of a moment.

"God, I've missed you."

"I've missed *you*—and I've been worried." She caressed his cheek as she searched his face wondering if he still didn't look a bit pale, but that could be the few pounds he'd lost. "Are you *really* better?"

"You're going to find out."

Resentful of the outerwear that kept them too far apart, Eve hugged him tighter as he greeted her with a kiss that almost erased the memory of several lonely nights. She wondered how someone could become such an integral part of your life so quickly. Every day she grew increasingly certain that what Derek had confessed to her about "falling" was happening to her, too. But what continued to leave her floor-flattened flummoxed, was how Sam not only threw away their relationship, but dishonored a man that she had to know would stand head and shoulders above others in principle and devotion to the woman he loved?

"You keep stroking me like that," he said, "and I'm going to start purring like the biggest house cat you ever saw."

Holding her hands up in surrender—one of which held the wine—Derek set it on the nearest flat surface and helped her remove her coat. When he saw her sleek, black cocktail dress, he whistled softly. "Who are you? This isn't my Evie…this is definitely *Lady* Eve."

The words were tribute enough. Added to the respect and desire she saw in Derek's gaze, and Eve was filled with hard-won pride. "Well, you know some of Rae's influence had to rub off eventually. Did I tell you that she made the Denver paper's Top Ten Best Dressed list?"

Trapping her face between his hands, Derek compelled her to meet his eyes. "This once, accept this as your achievement. A beautiful dress on a mannequin is what it is—well-cut and tailored cloth. A beautiful dress on an elegant and sophisticated woman is art for the senses, as much as the eyes. You're breathtaking…and I never wanted you more."

They feasted on each other as though they'd just discovered kissing. Their hands became instruments for sensory satisfaction and their murmurings to each other spoke to their appetite and need. When Eve finally realized that he'd only dragged on his ski jacket over his bare torso and had shoved his bare feet into jogging shoes, she paused in dismay.

"You've just been ill. Are you trying to catch pneumonia now?"

"No, a mermaid that I was foolish enough to let out of my sight for too long. She's turned into a goddess. Way above my pay grade."

With a pure "Evie" grin, Eve challenged, "Try me."

Derek drew her to the bedroom, his gaze never leaving her. The bed was already turned down, and the impression of his head was on the pillow. That confirmed Eve's suspicion that he'd been lying down here when she'd called. The blue-and-green striped comforter was flung half off the bed, indicating how anxious he'd been to get to the door.

"I did wake you," she said with mild reproach.

He began lowering the zipper of her dress. "I'll sleep even better now that you're here."

She didn't argue with that, and she didn't try to help him with her clothing because she was busy getting him out of his jeans. In the last second she checked his pockets.

"Uh-oh." Finding no foil packets, she observed, "I should have stopped at the apartment to pick up the sea urchin."

Except for the amusement and passion lighting his gray eyes, Derek managed to keep a straight face as he drew her gown and bra down her arms and below her breasts. "Any special effects you want to try," he said, lowering his mouth to her, "I'll be supplying them."

Chapter Eight

"Correct me if I'm wrong, but am I seeing strobe lights?"

Derek lay on his side, a glass of wine in hand, watching Eve tracing imaginary light patterns on the ceiling with her finger. That was in between dipping said index finger into her wine glass to moisten her lower lip.

"Well, if they're not, we're going to have to try again," he drawled, already willing. Then he frowned as he realized that she might not be doing that provocative move just to tease him. "Hey, did I hurt you?"

"It's not much. Doesn't alcohol kill germs? It's not like I have time to go for a tetanus shot."

As Derek's insides knotted at the thought of doing anything to mar her or cause her pain, the look she slid him was pure vixen and adorable. With a growl growing in his chest, he lunged at her. She yelped and sat up to put down her glass. Then she rolled onto her tummy to snuggle closer to him.

"Gotcha."

Yes, she had, and probably not for the last time, Derek thought. "I have a feeling gray hairs will be coming in fast and furious from here on."

But as he received her not-so-remorseful kiss of apology, he acknowledged the truth; Eve was putting "light" back into the concept of daylight for him, and turning his nights into something far richer and more fulfilling than the vacuous space of time he had to kill before returning to the office.

"So how was the meeting? Did you bewitch the film festival people, too?" He recalled from what she'd told him over the phone that the group would include a movie icon, an independent movie producer and the head of the city arts league, among others.

With a roll of her eyes, Eve admitted, "I felt like a duckling in a shark tank. But Rae was in her element. She simply enthralls. In a matter of seconds, she can figure out who to treat like a child with ADHD, and who needs facts or figures before they can show you any respect."

"You didn't feel comfortable at all?" Derek asked, a little worried for her. How could it be that looking as confident and able as she did, and exhibiting all of that with him, that she could still doubt herself?

Looking a little pleased with herself, Eve admitted, "In the end, I earned my dinner."

The sparkle in her blue eyes had him relaxing again. "I'm listening."

But she instantly demurred. "I don't want to talk shop. We haven't been together in days. *You* rarely say anything about work, except to tell me Landlord Ben is well—wherever he is. It's your turn."

Derek didn't want to talk shop, either. However, something had come up, and her surprise arrival had created an optimum opportunity to present an idea—or rather a request—to her. Optimum for him. His concern was over what her reaction would be. He could only hope that he wasn't about to jeopardize what they'd been carefully building between them these past weeks.

"There *is* something I'd like to talk about." He, too, set his glass down. "Actually, it's a favor to ask."

As he stretched out on his side to face her, Eve immediately began fingering the hairs on his forearm. "Uh-oh, I hear hesitation in your voice, G-man. Should I start worrying?"

"Probably."

Her bemused smile faltered.

"My boss, the Assistant Director, is flying in from Washington, D.C., next week, on his way to the West Coast for other meetings. He's bringing his wife," Derek added with a meaningful look. "I was hoping you might agree to help me entertain them."

"Gulp," Eve replied, with typical frankness. "I guess I shouldn't be surprised that this moment would come, but I honestly figured you would ease me into this escorting-hostessing stuff with another kidnapping to see Brad and Sophie? How about attending some wedding for one of your agents? I'm not ready to take on the big guns."

"He's only a grade or two above me."

"Only? And how long was it before I was

able to think of you as 'Derek' and not 'Special Agent-in-Charge Roland?'"

Her angst was palpable and Derek took her hand within his, wishing he could postpone this for her. But he had no control over management's schedules. "I knew this would send you into flight mode. I'm giving you as much time to prepare as I have myself. I only learned they were coming today."

"Can you really not solo this?" she asked, her gaze hopeful. "They don't have to know that you're in a—relationship."

Derek didn't miss how she almost stumbled over the word. "Inevitably the subject will come up. Once it does and it appears you're trying to hide the person, that starts the rumor mill. The last thing you need career-wise are rumors.

"The thing is that while Quentin and I would have meetings Friday and possibly a good part of Saturday, it would be a courtesy to a superior for his wife to be well taken care of while in an unfamiliar location. I'd hoped you could show Vanessa around on Saturday—take her shopping to a few places unique to the area and have lunch somewhere atmospheric. Then the four of us would do dinner in the evening. Quentin and I have known each other for almost as long as Brad and I do."

"Good grief," Eve moaned. "Even their names sound upper-tier society. I'll bet that their ancestors didn't only come over on the *Mayflower*—they owned the thing and the franchise on the ale and potato concessions."

She might be a bundle of nerves, but Derek was relieved to see she was trying to keep her sense of humor in check. "I'll admit that the Tamblyns get around in the social scene back East, but that shouldn't intimidate you as much now. You've been learning at the hands of a pro, Eve, and from everything you've told me, you're rubbing elbows with the who's who in

Denver and elsewhere with increasing regular-
ity. You've just confirmed as much with your
dinner meeting tonight," he reminded her with
a reassuring look.

"I talk too much. From here on, I'm taking
a page from *your* book, not marketing-meis-
ter Rae's."

"The point is, *wise guy,* if you can summon
the confidence for that, I know you can do
this."

Eve wagged her finger at him in disagree-
ment. "Rae would never send me out cold tur-
key, which is really what this calls for. Even
then she would forgive me if I committed a
faux pas or stuck my foot in my mouth a time
or two. Something tells me that there's a little
more pressure in your world. I don't want to
be the cause for you getting a bad report."

"I have total faith in you." That said, Derek
knew he had to be honest with her. "There is
just one more thing."

Eve's tinkling laugh spoke to her having reached her saturation point. "Let me guess— did Vanessa and Sam go on mani-and-pedi dates together?"

She might not yet have the confidence he wished for her, but Derek admired how quickly she caught on. "It would be wise to assume that they still do keep in touch."

Without a sound, Eve dropped her face onto the bedding.

"I'll give you as much background information on her as I can," Derek said, leaning over to kiss the top of her head.

"*No.* No!" Eve sat up, gulped the last two inches of wine in her glass, and started reaching for her clothes. "If you're into torture, I spotted a jar of honey in the pantry. Just pour the stuff over me and throw me on an ant pile."

While the honey idea triggered Derek's imagination, he was thrown by what she was doing. "Isn't that a little melodramatic? Eve?"

With a speed that had her gasping, Derek plucked her panties out of her hands and tossed them farther out of reach. Then he swept her across his lap. "Where do you think you're going?"

"Home."

"Not in this weather."

"And it'll be so much better in the morning? I don't want to stay here feeling as I do."

That sent Derek's heart pounding. "How do you feel?"

"You said you would never throw Wes in my face and trusted me not to use Sam against you, but you didn't have to seduce me to try for payback. You could have just said, 'Hey, Evie, how about we rub their faces in it for a change?' I would have said the same thing I'm saying now—'Thanks but no thanks,' but at least it would have been more honest."

Derek felt the blood drain from his face. "How can you believe this is anything other than what it is? Me in a bind. I told you, the Tamblyns don't need to know that we knew each other in Texas."

Although she flinched at his question, Eve held her ground. "You can't be serious. You won't be gone one minute before she starts giving me the third degree. Once she knows I'm from Texas, too, how long do you think it'll be before she has enough reason to dash for the ladies' room and calls Sam. I'll bet she does before you and the Field Marshall clear security in the Federal Building.

"Do you really not know how women can be to other women? And Sam may be married to Wes, but in her heart of hearts, she wants to believe that at least a little part of you is pining for her and always will."

"She's not that obtuse."

"Neither am I. This can't possibly be a smart thing for me to agree to, Derek. Now, please, let me go. I'm not going to put myself into a situation where I'm chewed up and spit out for the entertainment of someone who won't care to look at the facts."

"If that looks even remotely like it will happen, call me."

Eve twisted off his lap to be able to stare at him. "That would be the dumbest thing I could do—second to agreeing to this fiasco. Whine to you."

"I love you," he said quietly. "I wouldn't expect you to have the best time of your life, but I wouldn't put up with you being insulted, either."

At first Eve's eyes grew round…then they filled with tears. "How could you?" she whispered.

He'd just given her his heart and that was all she had to say? "What? I shouldn't tell you how I feel?"

"Not like this."

This time she did manage to get off the bed

and snatch up her things. Then she ran into the bathroom and slammed the door shut.

Dragging in a deep breath, Derek followed more slowly, but when he heard the lock set, he had to sit back down. "Eve. Sweetheart, I'm sorry."

There was no sound from inside the bathroom.

Idiot, Derek thought, rubbing his face with his hands. Of course she shouldn't have heard those important words the first time at that moment. It sounded too much as a justification for him to ask for her help. But the facts were the same: he loved her. He wanted to spend the rest of his life with her. The kind of occasions he was scheduled to have with the Tamblyns was going to be an inevitable part of their lives. He fully believed that she was going to be wonderful at them, an asset in a way the Vanessas and Sams of the world could only hope to be. He thought she would have wanted to hear that.

Sighing from growing fatigue as much as his mistake, Derek dropped back on the bed and stared at the ceiling. When she came out, he would try again. This time he would get it right.

"Okay, so it wasn't the best timing."

Halting mid-sip, Eve slowly put down her coffee mug and sent Rae a reproving look. "Not only not the best, but possibly among the *worst* ways to tell a woman something so important. It begs the question of whether he even meant it," she added, half to herself. Her heart was breaking and her stomach was cramping, although that was also for a cyclical reason. She'd been so busy, she'd lost track of time.

"Now stop right there." Although she'd been initially sympathetic, Rae now looked adamant. "Derek loves you. He's already called here several times, and you've said yourself that he's filling your voicemail box."

That's because he was a competitor at heart, she thought, a government soldier and she'd outmaneuvered him. He'd fallen asleep while waiting for her, and she'd not only used that opportunity to sneak out of the bathroom, she'd managed to get her jacket and things, and had tromped in her ridiculous high heels through the snow to her SUV and gone home without waking him. The near frostbite she'd suffered, added to the stress, was probably why the cramps were so bad this time.

At the crack of dawn, he'd been at her apartment door, but she'd waited him out again. Only when the hour forced him to get to work and she saw his black SUV pull out of the complex, did she venture from the sanctuary of her apartment. But he'd continued to call—

her answering machine, her cell phone, the office phone—even Rae's extension!

"Could you please focus on what is important?" Eve asked her boss. "He could have said the words the moment I walked into the house, or on the phone the other evening after that bus almost qualified us as a *Ripley's Believe It or Not* statistic—" or the best time, she thought with her heart wrenching, as they'd climaxed making love last night "—not when he's trying to get me to take the boss's wife off his hands."

"Oh, darling." Rae watched the light for Eve's extension light up again, and she nodded meaningfully at her. Only when the light went out and the main office went quiet again, did she continue. "Do you think Gus has never given his mouth carte blanche over his head? And don't think I don't get upset when he does, but I also can see that it upsets him as much as it does me. Sometimes more."

"Gus may look like a WWF wrestler, but he's mostly teddy bear," Eve said, thinking of the burly man. "I'll bet he was darling when he told you that he loved you."

A funny look crossed Rae's face. "Pretty much—until the avalanche."

Eve didn't know whether to laugh or believe her. "Seriously?"

"We were up looking at the land he intended to purchase, where the house is now. He was stomping around in the snow pointing out this and that—mind you, the contract wasn't even written up yet, let alone the trees removed from the building site, and the big gorilla is finalizing floor plans. He wanted my input on architectural style, the placement of windows, the shade of wood stain... How did I know? All I could see were trees, and I certainly didn't know if he really had the money to build something of the proportions he was talking about. I was just along for a ride in the mountains because I liked him. I thought he liked me, liked the sex. Maybe I wasn't being my most cooperative," she said with a shrug. "Suddenly, he erupts and yells, 'I love you, damn it! Do you want the kitchen facing the view or the road?' Seconds later, there's this odd noise and…this whole shelf of snow across from where we stood just went sliding."

"Oh, my gosh." Eve pressed her lips together to keep from giggling, as much from the image, as Rae's colorful recollections. "Poor Gus. It sounds as though you had him totally flummoxed. I hope no one was hurt?"

"No, but I'm sure the timber futures dropped a few cents that day from oversupply." As her lips curved into a wry smile, Rae reached for her planner and flipped to March. "Next Saturday is the Kids of Serving Soldiers thing at the skating rink. What if we put Honor on that to free you up? All I'd have to do is push up a manicure to Thursday or Friday."

Eve focused on the opportunity for Honor first. "You're serious? She would love that. But—"

"But nothing. You said she's been much improved over the last two events you invited her to assist you with. As if I wouldn't notice," Rae added.

"She didn't have anything going on, and I appreciated the help." Eve waited for a cramp to pass and continued, "Rae—forget Honor for a second. Why are you going to reschedule your appointment, too?"

"Because I'm going to help get you through this visit with the terrifying Tamblyns. At least the Vanessa part. I suppose I could invite myself to your evening plans, but that would come off as too stage-mother-ish, wouldn't it? Besides, I'm not old enough to be your mother."

Eve overlooked the fact that Rae was basically taking over plans for the weekend for the larger point. "I have just spent over twelve hours trying to avoid Derek. What in that behavior suggests that I'm going to agree to that weekend?"

Instead of looking up, Rae clicked through her BlackBerry's address box, then pressed on a listing. "You're going to do it." As Eve began to protest, she put up her finely manicured index finger to momentarily silence her. "Tina! Just the person I was hoping would answer. It's Mrs. Grainger. What's the possibility of switching next Saturday's appointment to Friday...? Yes, March. For you, I'll skip lunch. Thank you, dearest."

"Rae," Eve began upon realizing her boss was in steamroller mode. "Don't think I don't appreciate this—"

"The man is entrusting you with his career. In five or ten years that could be Derek's position. Are you going to help or hinder that?"

Eve couldn't believe her. After listening to

her protests about why she didn't want to get involved with Derek, this was Rae's best argument—that if she was very lucky, she would reside at government central one day? "Rae—*really?*"

"Okay, forget that. Then think of how you felt when you thought Derek was out of your life forever. If you make him walk away this time, he may not come back a third. I'm not saying you're wrong in your reluctance to do this, but do we not deal with people who need character tweaks every day in this business? And what if you're wrong about her being a witch?"

"She's—Sam's—friend," Eve enunciated.

"We'll go to Cherry Creek North," Rae said, already moving on.

Of course, Eve thought sardonically. "In that case you'll have to come. I don't shop there enough for them to remember me...although that is where I bought the New Year's dress. Okay, and the black one I wore last night."

With a benign smile, Rae continued. "For lunch, I think we should go to Gus's club. It has one of the best views of the city, and it's the end of the season for them to serve that decadent torte with gold leaf over the chocolate icing."

As pain almost made it impossible for Eve to follow Rae's chatter, she bent over the arm she had protecting her abdomen. "I really need to get to my purse and take something for these cramps."

"Poor sweetie. I just finished with mine, so the others can't be far behind. The way we cycle, we're like a herd of farm animals." Rae reached into her drawer, took out a little plastic container and offered it to her. "You know your condition is part of what's making you overreact to all of this."

Popping two tablets and washing them down

with a swallow of her own tepid coffee, Eve shuddered, then replied through gritted teeth, "I don't have a condition, and I am not over-reacting."

"Hormones," Rae sang softly. "In a day or two when you're over the worst, let's slot a couple of hours to upgrade your wardrobe a little more. Your evening things are superb, but we could add a little dash to your day-wear."

Before Eve could retort with an opinion of what her mentor was doing to her bank ac-count, her cell phone started buzzing again. She began to turn it off when Rae stopped her.

"Take it. I'm stepping out to give Honor the good news and get this coffee replaced." When Eve handed her mug over with a look of challenge, Rae added, "If you think that's the least bit annoying, you'll be disappointed. I was about to offer because I love you dearly and I want you to feel better."

"If that were true, you'd tell me to go home," Eve mumbled.

"'When the going gets rough, the tough get going.'"

As she closed the door behind herself, Eve let out a mixture of sigh and growl. Then she stared at the screen that identified Derek. Just before the call went to the automatic message cycle, she pressed the proper icon and said with resignation, "I'll do it."

"Eve. Thank God. Are you all right?"

She wanted to ask, "What do you think?" but could almost hear Rae whispering "hormones" in her ear. Maybe, she thought—but there was a healthy dose of fear and dread mixed in there, too.

"I will be."

"Sweetheart—I'm sorry."

"I don't really want to talk, Derek. I need to work. Think. I just gave you my word. Can that be enough for now?"

"I don't want your word, damn it. I want *you.*"

It was hearing his anguish that finally breached the walls that Eve had reflexively begun to resurrect. Resting her elbow on Rae's desk and resting her forehead in her head, she exhaled shakily. "I'm just not feeling well. I'll be better tomorrow."

"You're sick?"

"No, just cramping. The cyclical type."

"Come to the house after work," he coaxed. "I'll make you soup and nuke a towel to put on your back or tummy. Or if you'll let me, I'll just hold you."

There was no stopping the tears that slipped over the rims of her eyes. He didn't consider himself a good patient, and yet he wanted to take care of her? This was the man she'd found irresistible from the moment he'd rescued her in Rae's kitchen.

"I'll get there as soon as I can," she told him.

* * *

When Eve arrived at the cottage that eve-ning, Derek finally took his first pain-free breath of the day. He knew that they weren't out of the woods by a long shot, but she had come, and that was a huge step from his per-spective.

He'd shoveled a path to the front door for her and met her halfway. She had a wry smile on her lips, but her eyes exposed her fatigue and shaky condition. He thought he'd even glimpsed a little shyness, so when he took her case from her, he put his arm around her and, pressing a kiss to her temple, walked her the rest of the way inside.

"You can't know how grateful I am that you're here."

"Didn't you learn to run in the opposite di-rection when women are like this?"

Beyond her impish humor, Eve sounded a bit confused by his receptivity of her state. He could guess why. "I used to be one of those men. I suppose it's the woman who makes the difference."

Once inside, Derek locked up, set down her case, and helped her off with her red parka. Beneath it, she wore a two-piece black velvet pajama set. "You made yourself comfortable at the apartment, I'm glad."

"Not very sexy, I know," she murmured.

"You'd tempt me wearing a hazmat suit." When he spread his arms, she went to him and he folded her close until her cheek rested against his heart. "Just as I thought, soft as a kitten."

"You feel so good, I think I could fall asleep standing up."

"I figured you'd get here about reduced to crawling on all fours. Where do you want to camp out? Couch or bed?"

"Oh…it's too early for bed. I'll only wake at ten or eleven and lie there fidgeting and keeping you from getting any rest." Eve glanced toward the kitchen. "Whatever you're busy doing in there smells like food for the soul. I can sit at the kitchen bar and keep you company."

Although Derek appreciated the gesture, her heavy-lidded eyes and the way she sounded, he figured she'd fall off the chair in a dead sleep when his back was turned and add a cracked rib to her misery. "When did the cramps stop? The backache?"

"It all comes and goes. Right now it's ignorable."

She would have to try harder to convince him. "You can see fine from the couch, and it'll be much warmer and comfortable. Plus it's still close enough to talk if you can keep your eyes open for that long."

When he navigated her there, she saw the blue blanket and pillows with crisp, white pillowcases already arranged for her, and she turned into him to hide her face against his chest. "Derek."

"I know, sweetheart. You're welcome. Now sit."

She did and he slipped off her black sheepskin boots setting them out of the way under the coffee table. Then he lifted her socked feet onto the couch and folded the blanket over her.

"Did you take something for the symptoms?"

"This morning. I hate the drugged feeling that I'm left with, plus they don't do much for my symptoms. Maybe a glass of wine would be more effective."

He nodded, his own thoughts running along a similar line. "Some of the ladies in the office swear by cognac."

"Do they now?" Eve's lips twitched. "Did you just happen to eavesdrop, G-man, or take a survey? You're determined to have tongues wagging, aren't you? And hearts breaking."

"It's information accidentally gleaned—and

it happened before the holidays." He leaned forward to plant a tender kiss on her lips.

"Okay, I'm game."

He poured a splash into a snifter and brought it to her.

She shuddered at its potency. "That'll either work or knock me out."

"You want that hot towel now?"

"Thanks, but as it is, your cognac is going to have me feeling as though I'm in a sweat lodge. You take care of your soup."

"I'm going, I'm going. Just holler if you need something."

He turned once while working in the kitchen and found her watching him. The next time, she was fast asleep.

It was an hour later when he carried a tray with two mugs to the couch. She looked wholly peaceful, and, yet, only about a quarter of the brandy was gone. Studying her, he ached to take her to bed, remove her clothes, and make long languorous love to her. Those days were coming, many, many of them. He hadn't lost her trust. This was where she wanted to be.

Carefully sitting beside her, he set the tray on the coffee table and stroked her cheek with the backs of his fingers. Before he could repeat the caress, she'd closed her hand around his. Only then did she open her eyes.

It was dark and he'd shut the mini blinds and turned on a lamp in the opposite corner of the living room, which was all they needed besides the light above the kitchen sink. "Hey, sleeping beauty. Time to eat a little."

"Have I been out long?"

"Only an hour."

"It feels like four." She scooted up to a sitting position and fixed the pillows behind her. That's when she spotted the soup. "It looks wonderful, but I could have come to the table—and how comfortable can you be?"

As she began to try to maneuver her legs

around him in order to make room for him to sit back against the couch, Derek stopped her. "This is perfect. Here." He handed her one of the mugs. "I should have asked if you like tortilla soup?"

"Love it. Every variation. This is great, I can warm my hands and sip, and eat the rest like a stew after." She tasted the broth and murmured her appreciation. "This is divine. You led me to believe that you couldn't cook, that your freezer in the apartment was full of frozen dinners!"

"That was a minor untruth, but for a good cause."

Nodding with new understanding, Eve replied, "And it worked." After another sip, she said, "Rae is going to help. With Vanessa."

"Bless Rae. The more I thought about it, the more the idea of leaving you alone with Vanessa bothered me."

"Thank you. Now, please, let's not talk about her any more tonight?"

"It's a deal. I'd much rather cuddle, and maybe make out a little."

Although she smiled at his speaking glance and her eyes grew flirtatious, Eve said, "You don't have to put yourself through that."

He found her concern for his discomfort endearing, "The real torture comes from thinking you don't want me to touch you, sweetheart."

Three hours later, after watching a movie together, Eve came from the bathroom where she'd changed into a simple white T-shirt over her velvet pajama pants, she slid into bed with Derek.

"Are you sure you'll be warm enough?" he asked, as he drew her back against him, her bottom spooned by his hips.

"You're as hot as a furnace. You could keep me and two more my size warm."

"Talk like that isn't going to improve the situation, and for the record, you're all the woman I need."

As he stroked her from hip to knee, Eve took his hand and brought it to her breast. "Could you? They're so sore the first day or two."

"Like this?"

His touch was gentle as he cupped the subtle weight of her, then caressed her nipple with his thumb. Eve couldn't help but moan. "Yes."

"I love your body," he murmured, continuing to soothe her. "I adore how I just look at you, and these grow taut. When we're in the shower, a pearl can't match the sheen of your skin."

Over and over he stroked her bringing her body to life and replacing the ache with pleasure. She was helpless to keep from pressing back against his erection that thrust against her. They had made out as he'd wanted, but as she'd worried, it had become increasingly difficult for him to ease back from that flash-point. Now Eve had a need and she turned her face to him seeking his mouth for relief from the ministrations of his hands.

"I love this sweet mouth," he said, brushing his lips around and around hers. "I can't get enough of your tongue stroking mine, as when I'm inside you, those lips are a sweet torment when you slide them down my body."

"Kiss me," she whispered.

"I'd love to. I love you."

She whimpered as he took possession of her mouth at the same moment he teased both of her nipples until she had to slip her hand down between her legs for release.

"Derek," she said, when she caught her breath. "I'm sorry. That's so unfair." She was still trembling.

"It's all right, little mermaid." He held her close and nuzzled her hair, his hot breath was fierce against her ear, and his heart pounded like a jackhammer. "To know I can take you to the same place you take me is a lover's dream."

But he had been all generosity at the cost of his own body's torment. How could she only take from him?

She eased around to face him, and stroked her fingers across his bold brow, his high cheekbone and strong jaw. "You've changed me. I realize that if we're in a room full of people, the first and only face I find myself looking for is yours.

"I love to watch you undress and see the man who steals my breath away. I know your strength." She stroked her fingers across his shoulder and down his arms and farther until she laced her fingers with his. "These hands are trained to do damage, and yet no hands have ever made me feel more treasured.

"And this," she murmured, releasing him only to caress his erection. "So much power.

So much passion. I'm only half real until you're inside me."

As she spoke, she kept tracing every inch of him. Delicate, careful, until she closed her fingers around him.

"Eve…"

"Yes. Show me," she said, watching his eyes drift closed as he moved against her. She stretched so that his hot breath seared her lips and tightened her fingers more.

Derek groaned and closed his hand over hers and took over the rhythm. "Harder, baby. Love me."

"I do. I always will."

In the last second, Derek opened his eyes and locked his mouth to hers, and then it was all sensation, and she drank his cry of release.

Chapter Nine

The gray morning didn't help Eve's nerves, although her heart lifted when she drove up to the JW Marriot Hotel at Cherry Creek on the first Saturday in March and spotted Derek just emerging from his own vehicle. At least that much of their planning had gone right so far. Due to their mutual obligations yesterday, they hadn't seen each other since Thursday and she drank in the sight of him. He looked extra crisp in his navy blue suit, white shirt and burgundy-and-silver tie.

The instant he saw her SUV, he flashed his badge to the valet, then pointed to his vehicle and Eve's. After fastening his jacket, there were further instructions, and she surmised that he was telling the attendant that their visit was brief and that the SUVs should be left close to the door while they picked up guests. Then with long-legged strides, he came to assist her. Behind him, Eve saw her valet start over, only to come up short as the first valet called him back to pass on their orders.

Derek's possessive smile turned into a low wolfish whistle when he saw her outfit. The short, deep-pink bouclé jacket over the black cashmere sweater, black leather pants and high-heeled boots was no shrinking-violet outfit. Accessorized with an artsy silk scarf of bold blues and pinks, and enough bling to make her jingle and flash when she walked, she looked like a hotel guest herself. No small thing, as this was one of the top-rated hotels in the country.

Touching his lips near her right ear, he quickly breathed in her scent and made a throaty sound. "You look like a thousand calories a nibble," he murmured, "and I'm starving."

"Say that in twelve hours or so and your order will come with personalized gift *un*-wrapping—on the house."

"There went another corridor of brain cells up in smoke." He took her hand and, with a tender, reassuring squeeze, led her to the lobby. "It's good to see you feeling more confident about this."

"If you believe that, I'm a better actress than I thought," Eve replied, in the same low-key tone. However, they were turning both male and female heads, and as she caught their reflection in various glass doors and windows,

Eve did note with pleasure that they made an attractive couple.

The marble-and-granite lobby carried geographic themes of Denver's location near the base of the Rocky Mountains, the way the amber lighting and fuchsia and Big Sky–blue furnishings captured the tones in sunrises and sunsets. A subdued hum of activity supported the visuals—the hotel was moderately active for an otherwise lazy Saturday midmorning. Nevertheless, Eve had no difficulty in spotting the Tamblyns, even as Derek squeezed her hand to signal their presence.

"Oh, my—Glenn Close or Meryl Streep could play her in a slasher film," Eve said, between lips locked into a pleasant smile.

"*Now* your AWOL sense of humor decides to show up?"

"Only for your ears, G-man, I promise."

The formal-looking couple in their late forties were standing by the directory. Quentin

Tamblyn had the worldly, yet restrained aura of a man who'd spent decades working in government channels but was beginning to show a hint of weariness. Or was there something else that he was weary of? His premature silver-on-pewter hair was complemented by his charcoal-gray suit, and he seemed only slightly less fit and trim than Derek. Vanessa appeared to follow the philosophy that the sun was full of toxins and either she hadn't seen daylight since puberty, or else there really were such things as vampires. The closer they came, the more Eve realized that Vanessa's makeup accentuated her pallor, as did the jet-black hair cut bluntly at her chin. On the other hand, there was no criticizing her power-red wool blazer over a black maxi-dress and flat-heeled boots. The woman had the tall frame and thin bones for the style. But if any degree of real warmth could radiate from the woman's North Atlantic–colored eyes, Eve couldn't spot it.

Sam, if you made a friend of this one, you're more of a reptile than I gave you credit for being.

In their last few steps, Quentin took his own step forward, already extending his hand to Derek, as he broke into an appreciative smile. In smooth transition, his gaze slid to Eve, and she found herself swiftly analyzed. She thought she saw surprise and interest, but Assistant Director Tamblyn was a fortress to himself.

As the men shook hands, Quentin said, "Yesterday I told you that the altitude agreed with you, but I can see there's a better reason for your improved state."

"There's no denying that." Derek placed his hand reassuringly at Eve's waist and began introductions. "Sir, may I introduce Eve Easton."

Eve extended her hand and said warmly, "Welcome to Denver, Mr. Tamblyn."

Quentin's pale blue eyes searched her face

like a laser, but his smile warmed. "Thank you, Ms. Easton, this is a pleasure. It's so good of you to offer to entertain my wife while we workaholics go after it."

Turning to Derek, she beamed, but her eyes signaled, *"Offered?"*

Quentin gestured to his side, although Vanessa remained a step out of his peripheral vision. Eve found that fascinating and wondered if that was to keep him from seeing that she didn't yet see a need to pretend to be friendly? Eve's heart sank for what that might portend, but she held her own social smile.

"Mrs. Tamblyn. That's a wonderful Dior bag," she said, noting the telltale *D* in the position of the stirrup. "With your discerning eye, you'll enjoy our boutiques here at Cherry Creek." Since Vanessa didn't pretend to want to shake hands—or do more than nod—Eve refocused on her husband. "How was your first evening here, sir?"

"Very agreeable," he said. "We did stroll a bit, but we ate in the hotel, which proved a satisfying decision. Derek tells me that you're an events planner and one of the people to know in town?"

"The assistant to the owner of the company, but, yes, sir, if it's happening in Denver, we have the who, what and how-much-it's-costing data—or know how to get it." She added to Vanessa, "You'll get to meet Rae Grainger shortly. She's invited us to her home and wants to join us for some shopping and lunch."

When Vanessa gave her a sour smile and murmured, "How nice," Eve knew the woman had made her first error in underestimation.

"We're lucky Rae is in town this weekend, aren't we, Derek?"

He caught on quickly. "Usually, Gus and Rae head up to their mountain mansion to unwind. Gus is one of the top builders in the state and designed the place in a Frank Lloyd

Wright style, but with a Gus twist, wouldn't you say, Eve?"

"That's astute considering that it was dark when you were up there," she said, mischief in her eyes.

"Well, Gus told me himself," Derek drawled.

Everyone laughed.

"It's a shame you and Quentin have your boring meetings, Derek," Vanessa said crossing to him to kiss his cheek. "It's been ages, and we barely began catching up yesterday."

He politely returned her embrace, but there was no kiss on the cheek.

"Twenty-two years and she still ignores that if it wasn't for the necessity of these meetings, there wouldn't be these marvelous side excursions." Quentin said that to a space between Eve and Derek, and Vanessa visibly bristled. "Well, you ladies have a good time for us and I look forward to seeing you later this evening, Eve."

"Me, too, sir. I think I can assure you your share of adventure. I told Derek that you'd really enjoy a look at the unique eateries downtown. He said you're quite the wine connoisseur and I've made reservations for us at Corridor 44, which is the only champagne bar in Denver, and Crú, which has three hundred wines from around the world. Both serve gourmet food, as well."

"You've done your homework, young lady. I'm flattered and definitely look forward to that."

Eve tried to hide her sudden desperation from Derek, but he was more attuned to her than she realized, and surprised her with a soft kiss at the corner of her mouth.

"Call if you need me," he said quietly, before heading for the exit with Quentin.

Bolstered, Eve gestured after them. "Shall we?" she said to Vanessa and began walking. "I thought we'd start with a quick tour of the city—I understand it's been a while since you've been here, and much has changed. By then the shops will have opened and we'll get Rae."

With the hint of a weary sigh, Vanessa began walking beside her. "That sounds fine."

Once they were in her SUV, Eve dealt with the inevitable small talk.

"Let me know if you need more heat or the seat warmer. You'll enjoy the Graingers' home—it has a southwest flare. Both were built by Gus. Do a Google search for Gus Grainger Construction when you return to Virginia. His houses are always one of a kind."

"You seem charmed by him."

The hairs stood up on her arms, and Eve wondered if the woman had actually had the gall to insinuate what she thought she had? "The Graingers are huge assets to Denver. Rae is as supportive of her husband's work as she is hands-on with her own company. It's a full schedule, and yet she's also an artist. What do you do, Mrs. Tamblyn?"

"Me? You mean do I work?" she said. "I'm too busy for pedestrian employment."

"I'm sure there are many responsibilities that come with being the wife of a man in Mr. Tamblyn's position. But what are your interests, your passions?"

"My satisfaction and self-esteem comes from chairing various organizations and committees."

"You must be very good at it. Do you have children?"

"No." For the first time since entering the vehicle, Vanessa turned to look at her. "What's your story, Ms. Easton?"

"Please, call me Eve." Inwardly, she felt her insides clench as she thought, *Here we go.* "I've been in Denver for a year."

"You're obviously not married."

"Divorced."

"Children?"

"Not at this time."

"I detect an accent."

"Every region has at least one. Mine is Texan."

"What a coincidence," Vanessa all but purred. "Derek's last post was in Texas."

"Yes, I know."

"How did you and he meet?"

"At the Graingers' New Year's party at their mountain residence." She pointed to the dark glass and beam structure to their left. "That's the new Federal Building."

Vanessa made no pretense of even looking in that direction. "I saw it yesterday coming in from the airport. How interesting that you and Derek have only known each other barely more than two months, yet you already seem quite comfortable with each other."

"I don't think that there's a written-in-stone timeline for such things," Eve said with far more equanimity than she felt. Could she already know about their past? Derek would have told her if the subject had come up.

"Exactly where in Texas do you come from?"

So much for hoping the human bloodhound would miss whatever scent she'd caught. Drawing a steadying breath, Eve pointed out a few other landmarks that were relatively new. Then she said, "My parents are living north of Houston now near our grandparents, but I was born and raised in Dallas. In fact, it won't surprise you at all to learn that my ex-husband and I lived next door to Derek and Samantha."

Vanessa couldn't hide her satisfied reaction. "But you said that you two met for the first time this past New Year's."

"No, I said we met there. I never used the word *first*." And it would take water boarding to get her to admit the surprise of her life— that they had also discovered they were again neighbors for a time at the apartment complex.

"I adore Sam."

"I wish I could say the same thing. But it is a stretch to ask someone to feel warm and fuzzy toward someone that was sleeping with your spouse while pretending to be your friend."

"That's not the story I was told."

"I'll bet it wasn't."

"Is that why you went after Derek? A little tit for tat?"

Eve raised her eyebrows, but kept her focus on the road—the road she'd decided to turn onto that would take them to Rae's. She could only hope that in the presence of another person Vanessa Tamblyn knew when to shut up.

"Mrs. Tamblyn, I take exception to that remark."

"That would be my strategy, too, were I in your shoes. After all, what other option do you have?"

The audacity of the woman! Eve couldn't help but laugh in disbelief. "I don't need an option, I have the truth, and I don't owe it to you or anyone else." Why bother trying, when clearly Vanessa had her mind made up? Heaven knows, Sam had undoubtedly established her own "history of events" that would cover her adulterous and despicable behavior, and there were always plenty of Vanessas in the world to assume an allegation was gospel because it suited their personal prejudice or agenda.

"The happy couple are expecting, did you hear?"

"Derek did. We wish the child every happiness."

"Well, one thing you can't take away from Samantha," Vanessa said with pride, "she's raised Wes's stock greatly. There's talk about him running for mayor."

Eve almost choked. If it wasn't about football, basketball or baseball, you would have to all but put Wes on a leash to get him into a meeting. What rocket scientist thought he had the interest or qualifications to run for mayor? "Well, he better hope he has enough connections to have his voting record buried," she said drolly. "When people discover he usually used a ballgame or a practice to get out of performing his civic duty, his lack of citizenship is bound to underimpress voters."

That silenced Vanessa for the rest of the trip to Rae's house. The house itself had her lips parting as she gasped softly. "That's quite beautiful."

Rae opened the door with great fanfare and welcomed them, all graciousness. The house was already decorated for spring, despite some snow lingering in spots on the lawn. She had an elegant, but whimsical eye for decorating, so bunnies and baskets filled with glass and hand-painted eggs were strategically placed to enhance or amuse. Pots of hyacinths and tulips, daffodils and narcissus added to the beauty of the rich earth tones throughout the house.

"My, this is amazing," Vanessa said, her gaze roaming. "You're very talented, and I love your colors."

"You're too kind." Behind Vanessa's back, Rae winked at Eve. "I wish we had time to show you our other place, but shopping beckons. Let's take my car, then Eve won't have to listen to me navigate, even though she knows all of these spots herself."

Eve knew better. Rae drove an exquisite white Mercedes with matching leather interior, and was undoubtedly thinking it would help her rapport with Vanessa to chauffeur her around in first-class style. Little did she know, Eve thought.

"Might I use the powder room first?" Vanessa asked Rae, with a warmth she'd yet to exhibit this morning.

"Of course. Forgive me for not offering my-self." Rae pointed to the nearest door.

As soon as the door was shut she turned to Eve with a worried expression. "Love the outfit, not so much the tension you're emanating."

"Then do us both a favor and keep all sharp objects out of my reach until we drop her off at the hotel."

"That bad?"

"I wish there was time to tell you, but just know I owe you big time for coming along today."

Fifteen minutes later they were at Cherry Creek North, the boutique center of Denver that consisted of twenty city blocks of stores, of which approximately forty were unique to the area.

"We'll just get started, and then continue after a light lunch," Rae said. "Vanessa, is there something in particular you'd like to look for?"

"Not particularly. Everything looks so fresh and tempting, so please lead on and I'll happily follow."

It amused Eve that the first place Rae chose to take them to was where they'd found her jacket. The moment the owner spotted them, she came over to take Rae's hand in both of hers as she welcomed her back, then gave Eve a warm embrace. "Eve, you are better than an advertisement for us, and I love that ensemble. You look as though everything was cut on you. So good to see you again."

"Lovely to see you, Francesca. We're showing a VIP guest the best of Denver. Vanessa Tamblyn of the Washington, D.C., area, Francesca Loren."

"Welcome." After offering coffee, tea or an early taste of champagne, she encouraged, "Please, make yourselves at home and let us know if we can assist you."

There was no missing that Vanessa was filing every utterance and nuance away—undoubtedly to be reported to Sam, rather than Quentin, Eve thought—but she didn't begin purchasing anything until Francesca watched her reluctantly put back a bejeweled cardigan.

"If madam needs a smaller size, I think I have one in back, and as a friend of Rae and Eve, we're happy to gift you with our guest discount."

"You're so kind," Vanessa replied, pressing a hand to her heart. "In that case, please add those earrings I was just looking at to my purchases."

Lunch was another success, which Eve expected, since they did go to Gus's club. Rae was immediately recognized and welcomed with enthusiasm, and they were shown one of the coveted tables by the windows that looked out at the mountains.

Afterward, it was off for more shopping. At every stop, Vanessa ingratiated herself to

Rae and, of course, the shop owners and their staff. Otherwise, whenever possible, she ignored Eve.

"You do bring out the chill in some icebergs," Rae noted to Eve at one opportune moment. Vanessa was in a fitting room trying on more outfits.

"On behalf of icebergs, I resent that slur," Eve countered.

"How on earth are you going to get through tonight?"

"Prayer, Pinot Noir and G-man keeping a steadying hand on my thigh."

Four o'clock couldn't come soon enough, and Eve was additionally grateful that Rae suggested they drop off Vanessa at the hotel. She reasoned that it was closest, although in actuality it was pretty much the same either way.

As soon as they were merging with traffic again, Rae uttered a diaphragm-deep roar. "Would you believe that she-cat actually tried to start trouble between us by asking if I noticed how you would pull store managers and owners aside after you would talk to them and contradict something I said, or try to curry special favor for yourself?"

"That always works," Eve said dryly. "Because those very people would *never* think to call you and warn you about me. I've got you all just where I want you."

"But the truth is she's the one who was conniving," Rae continued. "After Francesca's generosity, Vanessa was telling everyone else about what she was doing and they felt strong-armed into matching that."

"I apologize for getting you involved in this," Eve said, reaching over to touch her shoulder.

"Is her husband too busy being a creep, himself, to notice what she's like?"

"He seems like a good man and, probably—as with Derek and Sam—he's trying to lose himself in his work and hope that there's a reprieve somehow, someday soon."

"What a wasted life." Rae grimaced as though she'd tasted something bitter. "Just be careful. Please."

Eve was entering her apartment when Derek called.

"How are you? Home yet?"

"The dead bolt is secured, the boots are about to come off and, since we'll be doing wine tastings this evening, I'm heading for a soothing shower to avoid imbibing. But I'm tempted to pop a cork, believe me."

"Uh-oh," he replied. "The fact that you didn't disconnect once you saw it was me calling gave me hope things weren't as bad as you feared they would be."

"Feel free to call Rae for a confirmation if you need it."

"Damn...sweetheart, I'm sorry." With a

heavy sigh, Derek added, "I'll shower and change myself and be there shortly. You can fill me in on everything."

An hour later, she opened the door to him and he quickly drew her into his arms. He had changed into a suede-gray sports jacket, gray slacks, a silvery white shirt and a white-on-silver tie. He looked and smelled every bit as good as he felt.

"I'm sorry for putting you through this." He pressed his face against the side of her neck as his hands moved up and down her back as though it had been days instead of hours since he'd seen her.

"The accusations she made, the twisted fabrications…"

"Tell me."

Eve did, until she couldn't remember having left anything out. Through it all, Derek grew more furious.

"We'll cancel dinner. I'll talk to Quentin. He has to understand. Hell, he has to *know*. Even I wasn't clueless that Sam wasn't up to any good."

"No," Eve replied. "We'll get through this. I can do it, now that you're here. I'll just avoid being alone with her, that's all." She stroked his freshly shaven jawline. "I missed you so."

He kissed her before she could say anything more. It was a kiss of reverence that quickly built into hunger. "I'm sorry for messing up your lipstick, but I needed that." He took a deep breath and stepped back to take in her outfit.

Eve had styled her short hair into a more punkish-whimsical fashion, added a bit of drama to her eye makeup, and was wearing a one-shouldered, black lace cocktail-dress that emphasized her small waist and shapely legs.

Derek drew her back into his arms. "You may have managed to surpass the New Year's dress. Although your tush in those leather pants almost caused some head-on collisions among pedestrians."

Laughing softly, she then stroked her hand over his chest. "You're looking very sexy yourself."

"I didn't want you to think I had only one look—government."

Eve wrapped her arms around his neck. "It won me over, didn't it? Kiss me one more time before I fix this face."

"I thought you'd never ask."

When they arrived at the hotel to pick up the other couple, the Tamblyns weren't yet downstairs. Eve and Derek waited by the elevators, one of which opened to the scene of Vanessa and Quentin on the opposite side of the car, both of their faces set in stony expressions.

Quentin wore the same suit, but had changed to a salmon-colored shirt and darker tie, while Vanessa was in a teal tunic-and-skirt set that was striking against her coal-black hair. Tonight she was wearing opaque hose and heels and she was carrying a black cashmere wrap she'd purchased today.

"Hello, everyone," Eve said, forcing herself back into performance mode. "Vanessa, that's a fantastic color for you."

"Thank you. Good evening, Derek, dear."

He merely nodded to her, but to Quentin he offered a more conversational, "Are you ready to share your expertise in wines?"

"We're going to Larimer Square," Eve explained to both of them. "Specifically Corridor 44 and Crú."

"Eve was telling me about it at lunch today. You're going to love it," Vanessa assured her husband, with an awkward smile.

Quentin gestured to encompass Eve and Derek. "With this company, how could I not?"

The proverbial pin didn't drop, and it was a silent walk to Derek's SUV.

Corridor 44 was a sexy champagne bar with white booths. There were witty and wise quotes painted on the walls by the likes of Noel Coward and Winston Churchill. By then the atmosphere between Vanessa and Quentin had eased somewhat and Derek was able to draw Quentin into conversation. Along with their wine choices, Eve and Derek chose to share a half dozen oysters after he teased that he was tempted by the oyster shooters. Vanessa went with the caviar, and Quentin ordered the tuna crudo with edamame salsa.

Although Vanessa's face tightened when Derek attentively assisted Eve in the removal of her cape, Quentin was complimentary of her attire and a true gentleman. That, too, didn't sit well with Vanessa. Thankfully, the champagne arrived quickly.

"Has this guy told you how he got his nickname in the agency?" Quentin asked Eve, after conversation about the vintage of the wine was fully exhausted.

She looked from the distinguished man to Derek. "I didn't know he had a nickname."

"Some try to keep theirs from friends and family," Quentin explained with a wry smile, "but just about everyone ends up with a handle."

Eve lifted her eyebrows at Derek in silent query. She wasn't going to put him on the spot if he didn't want to play along, but she couldn't deny she was curious.

After sending a thanks-for-nothing look, he qualified the story by explaining, "I was relatively new with the Bureau. We were down in the Florida swampland tracking down a good lead on a drug runner, but what seemed like a promising lead, led to nothing. It was getting dark and a storm was blowing in.

"We'd seen several alligators while out cruising through the marsh, so you can imagine that when we got out of the motorized raft and bent to help haul it farther up to our vehicles, when someone yelled, 'Gator!' I spun around and pretty much annihilated a chunk of tree trunk a few yards behind me. Ever since then I've been known as Gator."

Eve couldn't help but chuckle; however, she leaned against his shoulder and patted his leg, as well. "That makes all the sense in the world to me. I would have been dubbed, Walks with Damp Denims."

That earned another laugh, until a bored-looking Vanessa excused herself to go to the restroom.

After that they moved on to Crú, which was designed around lots of wood. Black tablecloths adorned the tables and they advertised at least three hundred different wines.

Quentin seemed to enjoy sharing his expertise more this time—or else he was better acquainted with the labels. Eve found him a talented storyteller and was grateful that he kept them all entertained through the various steak dinners that they'd chosen.

When it came time for the check, Eve decided it was her turn to excuse herself and located the ladies lounge. She had just started her return when Vanessa came straight at her. There was a glint in her eye that had Eve thinking about Rae's warning.

"I just want to tell you that I think you're a little fraud," the taller woman said. "I believe Sam when she says that it was you and Derek who acted badly."

"Vanessa," Eve said, as a couple exiting gave them wider berth. "We made it through a difficult weekend. Why not go on with your trip and your life, and don't mind other people's business?"

"Because I'm a good friend. I will not stand

by and let you succeed." Her voice took on a more ominous tone. "You know I can see to it that Derek's reputation is ruined. The correctly placed word here, and innuendo there, and he'll never see another promotion—thanks to you."

"Derek is the most honorable man I've ever been privileged to know," Eve said with resolve. "Whether his career continues to flourish or flounder, I'll be right by his side if he wants me. But as for threatening a fine man's career—perhaps you should consider how your husband would take that."

"He needn't ever know," Vanessa replied with contempt.

"But I already do," Quentin said, directly behind her.

Stricken, Vanessa turned to find Derek standing right beside her husband. As she opened her mouth to speak, he raised his hand.

"Not another word." To Derek, he said,

"You've been through enough. We'll catch a cab. Thank you for what was primarily an enjoyable night."

They shook hands, and then Quentin circled his wife and came to Eve. He took her hand in both of his. "Forgive me for not sparing you this. I hope we meet again."

"Me, too, sir," Eve whispered, shaken and hurting for him. She watched as Quentin took Vanessa's arm and led her out, and then slumped against Derek when he put his arms around her.

"It's over," he said softly.

"Should I have at least been fair and told her you two were standing behind her?"

"She set her own trap. She deserved what happened." He pressed a kiss to the center of her forehead. "What you said about me—if you didn't already own my heart, I'd have lost it to you then."

"Well, darn," she muttered, pretending to

be exasperated. "A wasted compliment. Can't you...*double* love me or something?"

"We can go home and figure something out."

Eve laced her fingers through his. "My G-man."

Epilogue

On the first Sunday in June, Eve and Derek flew to Texas for the christening of three-month-old Evagail. Sela had asked Eve to be her godmother, and along with the honor, Eve was excited to introduce Derek to her family.

They were all there in the nondenominational church after regular services—four generations of the clan and assorted other guests. Eve thought there had to be at least sixty present, and she didn't recognize half of them, but she thought that was wonderful, too. In a world of so much sadness and pain, it was good to celebrate life.

Through the brief ceremony, little Evagail behaved like an angel and looked the part in the long white gown she'd been allowed to buy for her. Her brother Nicholas was made god-father, and he spent the service with his arm around her, clearly moved by the moment, too.

Afterward, as Eve passed the baby to Sela, she went to Derek standing apart and observing the scene. "Why are you way over here? They won't bite."

"I know. I was enjoying the view." Stroking her arms, he looked deeply into her eyes. "What if I said that I want the next baby you hold to be ours? Would you need much time to get used to the idea?"

Overwhelmed, Eve threw herself against him and whispered, "Derek!"

The family returned to the Easton home, and things grew hectic for a while as the kids chased through the house, the women set to work with final preparations for lunch and the men collected on the front porch. When she saw there was plenty of female help in the kitchen, Eve went to find Derek. Since his question in the church, she couldn't bear not being able to look at him, to touch him. But he wasn't on the porch.

"Where's Derek?" she asked her brother-in-law Mitchell.

He pointed with his beer bottle to one side of the house, then the other. "Ah...well, Pop was showing him his new golf cart. I guess they went farther than I realized."

Much farther. It turned out that the two men didn't reappear until the dinner bell on the front porch was rung. Her father passed her and she pinched him.

"Where on earth were you going, all the way to the golf course?"

"Well, I drove some, and Derek wanted to

try it." Her father kissed her cheek. "It's fried chicken and salads—what's going to taste bad cold?"

Derek brought up the rear and stopped a step down to where she was almost face-to-face with him when he wrapped his arms around her waist and held her against his chest. "Did anyone tell you that you're the prettiest thing here?"

Although she liked her white suit, she had to protest this time. "Christenings follow the traditions of weddings. No one is ever more beautiful than baby."

"Baby, baby," he crooned against her lips.

When they joined the family around the table, Eve's heart was still racing from Derek's kiss. She wasn't quite paying attention when her father stood and began the toast to Sela and Mitchell, and of course Evagail.

"It would appear that our family is going to continue growing—even faster than anticipated," he began. "Derek has asked me for our blessing in marrying our Evie." While he squeezed the shoulder of Eve's mother, who immediately began to weep, he added, "Of course, fine man that he is—and fool that I'm not—I did just that."

Eve turned to Derek and her own eyes filled. "That was so sweet of you to think of such a tradition."

Nicholas called from several seats over, "I don't see any ring."

Eve sent him a quelling glance. How like him to try and ruin a precious moment. Then she heard a series of "oohs" and "ahhs" and turned back to Derek who was on his feet reaching into his pocket. That had her catching her breath.

"I happen to have it right here." He went down on one knee and took her hand, asking, "Eve, I love you. I long have, and I always will. Will you marry me, share your family and heart with me?"

"Yes," she whispered.

Amid cheers and tears, she felt him slip the ring on her finger. But it was some time—after more kisses and many hugs from her family—that her vision cleared enough to actually see the emerald-cut diamond with the three smaller stones on either side. She could only stare at it and him, incredulous, as questions raced through her head. When did he do that? How had he known the right size?

"Mommy!" Eve's youngest nephew, Hayden, demanded from the other side of the table, breaking into her dazed euphoria. "Does that mean Uncle Derek's toofbrush is gonna move and be neighbors to Aunt Evie's toofbrush like yours and Daddy's did?"

Amid the hoots of laughter, Derek grinned at Eve and replied, "Neighbors again. Definitely!"

* * * * *